I Won't Give Up On You

F. L. Jacob

I Won't Give Up on You
Copyright 2014 by F.L Jacob

Cover Design by Michael J. Mitchell of Digital Mitchell Photography
https://www.facebook.com/digitalmitchell

Editing by Book Peddler's Editing
https://www.facebook.com/BookPeddlersEditing

Interior design by Fictional Formats
https://www.facebook.com/Fictionalformats

ISBN-13: 978-0692024225
ISBN-10: 0692024220

Dedication

I dedicate this book to everyone who has been there for me the last few years. All the ups and downs, the tears, the laughs.

Thank you.

I promise you, I won't give up.

Author's Note

I highly recommend reading book one, *Have I Told You*, before reading this book. *I Won't Give Up on You* is a continuation of the story line that was started in *Have I Told You*.

Please remember this book is for readers 18 years and older. It contains sexual encounters and graphic language that some readers may find questionable. The book is not suitable for anyone under the age of 18.

Prologue

Caston

Arriving in the ER we were immediately swarmed by nurses and my hand was torn from Sabrina's grip. My mind was a jumble as I tore through the halls frantically trying to get answers. I had never seen so much blood.

"Why the fuck is she still bleeding? Where's the fucking doctor?" I screamed as I paced the hall.

"Please, move out of the way, Mr. Black. We must get her up to surgery. She is losing too much blood," a doctor in blue scrubs and a plastic mask said.

I was able to grasp her hand as they wheel her past me on the way to the elevator. I squeezed it as hard as I could. Our eyes met, my heart was ripped from my chest. She looked so scared.

"Don't give up on me, baby." I whispered in her ear just as our hands were being pried apart by the nurses. I sank to my knees as the elevator shut in my face. *Sabrina, please be okay. I can't live without you.*

Chapter One

Caston

I paced the sterile halls of the hospital's surgery wing. Sabrina lost so much blood she was rushed away to surgery to stop the bleeding and repair the damage as soon as the ambulance arrived at the hospital. Watching her slip from my fingers as they wheeled her away from me made me realize I wasn't in control of what was happening, and it scared me. My fiancée was in trouble, and I couldn't help her. I felt hopeless and alone.

Jon and Sara were still in the ER getting their injuries from the kidnapping and beating assessed. Whoever helped Beverly had done a number on them.

I stopped at the end of the hall and leaned up against the wall, letting my head fall back against the smooth surface. I sent up a silent prayer. I needed my love to make it. I wouldn't be able to live without her.

Looking down at my hands I noticed that they were still stained with Sabrina's blood. My shirt was a mess too, but I couldn't leave, I couldn't risk missing an update from the doctors. I shook my head to rid myself of the idea that I might not see Sabrina again. Taking a deep breath, I unbuttoned the cuffs of my shirt and rolled up my sleeves as I slowly made my way to the waiting area. I was the only one in there. Thankful for the quiet and privacy, I sank down into the chair at the end of the row. It was ugly olive green leather with wooden arms, hard and uninviting. I sat and stared into space. I was so wrapped up in what was going on with Sabrina that I had no thoughts. My mind was blank for once in my life.

Hearing the door creak, I stood up and quickly turned around. A nurse stood in the doorway with something in her hands. She was about five feet two inches and blond. Completely opposite of Sabrina, but she had a warm smile and apologetic eyes.

"Mr. Black?" she whispered.

I nod. "Yes, is there any news?" I asked, hoping she would be able to share any information she might have.

She looked down at the floor and said, "No, I'm sorry, I don't have any updates. I just wanted to give you these." She walked toward me and held out the package she carried. "It's nothing really, and don't feel obligated to use them, but I saw your clothes were ruined, and I thought you might like something to change into."

I reached for the package and opened it to find scrubs. "Thank you for your thoughtfulness."

"You're very welcome, Mr. Black. Is there anything I can do for you before I go back?"

The flush of her skin made me uneasy. "No, thank you, uh," I paused not knowing her name.

"Candy, my name is Candy."

Turning away from her, I mumbled under my breath, "Of course it is."

"Excuse me?" she said as she leaned over to see if she could see my facial expression.

"Nothing. I'm fine, thank you. Oh, and thank you for the clean clothing."

She blushed again and turned to walk out of the room.

I sat back down on the uncomfortable chair and waited.

It had been a few hours and still no one had come to update me on Sabrina's status. I heard some commotion at the doorway. I turned just as the doors flung open. Sara and Jon came barreling into the room, only to freeze when they saw me.

It felt like the seconds lasted minutes, hours even, as we stared at each other not knowing what to say.

Finally, Sara rushed over to me, and I caught her in my arms. "Caston, have you heard anything yet?" Tears rolled down her face.

As if on cue the other set of doors swung open and a group of doctors, talking among themselves, walked in. We turned to face them, and it was so quiet you could've heard a pin drop. I felt as if my heart would fall out of my chest.

"Mr. Black?" The lead surgeon stopped a few feet in front of the team who sought me out.

My voice disappeared on me. "Yes?" I finally managed to get out.

"She's in recovery, and then will be moved to the ICU. There was a lot of blood loss, and we had to do multiple blood transfusions. The artery in her leg was nicked by the bullet. That's what caused the bleed out. We were able to stop it, but there were some complications."

I felt my legs give out as I dropped to my knees, but Jon was at my side before I hit the ground. He helped to keep me standing as I listened to the rest of the news.

"Her blood pressure dropped several times, and she went into cardiac arrest once. We were able to bring her back, but she's in a coma. I'm not sure if there will be any permanent damage and, right now, I'm not sure if she will even wake up. We take it day by day now. I'm very sorry I don't have better news for you."

Jon, knowing I wasn't in the right state of mind, asked, "When can we see her?"

"Probably in an hour or so. Someone will come and get you in the waiting room on the ICU floor. I just want to warn you that she looks pretty rough."

"Thank you, doctor." Jon reached out to shake the doctor's hand as I turned into Sara's open arms and sobbed uncontrollably.

Sara wrapped her arms around me and ushered me to the row of chairs again. Helping me sit, she took my face in her hands and wiped my eyes with her thumbs.

"Caston, focus, look at me. Baby, you have to settle down. Sabrina is a fighter. She'll make it. She won't give up, and I won't let you give up on her. Breathe, Caston. I need you to breathe."

Jon sat beside me, his hand rested on my back to offer support. "Caston, we're here for you, but you need to be strong for her."

I nodded, trying to catch my breath and get my emotions in check. Whispering to Sara as I gasped for air, "I can't lose her. She… she's… everything."

"I know, Cass, I know." Sara laid my head on her shoulder, and I cried even more.

We moved up to the ICU waiting area as soon as I felt my legs would hold me. As we took our seats, Jon left Sara and me to let the nurses know the family of Sabrina Bennett was in the waiting area.

He returned to the room with a couple cups of steaming liquid and handed them to us.

"Thanks, bro, but I don't like coffee."

"I know, its hot chocolate." He smiled. "I didn't forget you hate coffee. Sara doesn't like it either, remember? You guys are just weird."

We all chuckled and took a sip of our drinks. The hot liquid going down my throat did little to warm my body. I felt so cold and empty. We sat in silence, listening to the television in the corner of the room. I checked my watch; we'd been sitting here for too long with no update. Not being able to take it anymore, I stood up and threw my crushed cup in the trash.

"I can't take it anymore. I'm going to find her."

I took off down the hall before Sara or Jon could stop me. I pressed the button to be buzzed into the unit. Impatiently tapping my foot I paced in front of the double doors.

"Can I help you, sir?" A voice came through the speaker.

Sliding to the metal grate where the voice emanated, "Yes, please, I'm here for Sabrina Bennett."

Silence. It was killing me. Beyond frustrated, I hit the cement wall.

"Sir, I'm sorry you will have to come back tomorrow, visiting hours are over."

"Bull shit! I've been waiting all day. The doctors told me I could see her when she got into her room." I braced myself on the wall with the speaker between my hands.

No way they'd keep me from her, I'd move heaven and hell before I let them tell me I have to go home. Knowing money talks I pulled out my phone and started making calls. Eventually I reached the president of the hospital. I promised him a good deal of money toward a new wing of the hospital. Hanging up, I waited by the door for only a few seconds when it buzzed open. I quickly walked through the doors that led to the patient rooms. I was met at the door by a burly woman bearing a disgruntled face.

I once heard that when you find love, no matter what happens in life you will always be drawn back to that person. It was as if Sabrina's soul was talking to me. I turned to walk down the hall with the woman on my heels trying to stop me, going right to room 2621. Somehow, I knew she was in there.

"Sir, please. Stop you can't—"

I stopped at the door and look back to her face. She was really angry. "She's in here, isn't she?"

"Yes."

That's all the confirmation I needed. I pulled the sliding door to the side and walked in, drawing the curtain behind me. My breath caught in my throat. There she was, tubes came from her mouth and nose, IVs protruded from her arms, and the ventilator slowly pushed air in and out of her lungs. She looked so beat up and battered.

I couldn't even get close to her. My heart ached to see her like this. Noticing a chair on the other side of the room, I pulled it over next to her bed. I sat opposite the machine showing her vitals. The only noise was the rhythmic beeping. Carefully picking up her hand, I raised it up to my lips and placed a light kiss on one of the only spots that didn't have something sticking out of or attached to it. I was very careful to not disrupt anything. Taking a deep breath, I placed her hand back down and covered it with mine. Just being near her made me realize how much I wanted to be her rock. I'd give her all my strength to make her well if I could. Stroking my thumb over her skin made her heart rate slow slightly on the monitor. I leaned over and kissed it again; my touch calmed her. Moving my head to the right, I lay my head on the bed and stared up at her beautiful face.

My heart broke seeing her lay there motionless when not twenty-four hours ago we were wrapped in each other's arms. She had been so full of life and happy. Her smile lit me up, and she made me whole.

A nurse walked into the room and startled when she saw me. "I'm sorry, sir, I didn't think we let family in here yet."

My head didn't move from where it rested on the side of her bed. I stared at Sabrina, watching her chest move up and down with the ventilator. "You didn't... I couldn't stand it any longer. Mr. Bratten gave his approval for me to be here."

"Okay, but I need to get over to her to check her tubes and flush out her IVs. Could you at least step out for a minute or so?"

I sat up in the chair and nodded. Her smile was warm and sincere. I was thankful she would be taking care of my girl. Holding out my hand, I introduced myself. "I'm Caston. I'm sure we'll be seeing a lot of each other."

"Kelsey," she walked up to me to return the handshake. "Unfortunately, yes, I think we will. But you got the suite, so I'm sure she will be quite comfortable while she's with us."

Kelsey walked to the computer on the wall and turned it on, pulling up Sabrina's charts. As she went about her work, I decided I'd step outside and stretch my legs.

I remembered I left Sara and Jon in the waiting room a while ago. Putting my hands in my pockets, I skulked back to them.

It was well past midnight, and my body ached from the long grueling day of emotional highs and lows. Reaching the door way, I peeked in and saw Jon sitting on the couch staring at some unknown infomercial. Sara was stretched out, resting her head on his lap. He mindlessly stroked her hair. It was the first time I really looked at them since they appeared at my side downstairs.

Jon had a bandage on his head. He now had his arm in a sling. He hadn't had it on a few hours ago when they found me, even he was trying to be stronger. His knuckles were all cut up, and there were cuts on his cheek. Sara had bruises up and down her arms and legs. There were small cuts on her face too. Thankfully, they seemed superficial and unlikely to scar.

Walking in a little further, Jon looked up at me finally breaking his stare and held his finger up to his lips to remind me to stay quiet, so not to wake Sara. I nodded and took a seat a few spaces down from him.

"Did you see her?" he whispered.

I nodded. "She looks horrible, Jon. Why? Why did this have to happen?" I hung my head low, holding it up with my hands while I rested my elbows on my knees.

"Cass, Beverly is fucked up in the head. She's in jail now. There's no way they'll let her out. I'll make damn sure that won't happen again."

I looked up at him. "All I wanted to do was to make her my wife and grow old with her."

"And you will."

I managed a smile and then looked away because tears brimmed my eyes. Sliding my hands through my hair, I blew out a deep breath and leaned into the wooden arm of the chair to try to get comfortable. Feeling myself drift to sleep, I popped my head back up a few times. I didn't want to miss the nurse coming to get me.

Sleep won out because I woke to a warm hand on my shoulder. "Mr. Black, you can come back to the room now."

Looking at my watch it was almost morning. Jon still sat staring at the television. I was thankful they were still here for support, but I couldn't keep them here.

"Jon, why don't you take Sara home and come back later after you get rest. If there's any change I'll call you. From what they said it probably won't be today."

He nodded, looking as defeated as I felt. "Can we bring you something back, Cass?"

"No, just call me before you come back."

I walked over to Sara and placed a kiss on her temple.

I didn't leave Sabrina's side for days. Jon and Sara took turns coming to sit with me, bring me fresh clothing and paperwork that needed my approval. I was thankful my staff took over and kept all my businesses afloat.

Today was a particularly special day. The doctor determined Sabrina could be taken off the ventilator. I panicked with all the 'what ifs' going through my head. Dr. Dana came in for the procedure. She was very reassuring that everything would be okay. I sat in the corner of the room and chewed on my thumb while I watched them work on Sabrina.

My phone chirped, alerting me to a new email. I have never been so thankful to have the distraction. I grabbed my phone and excused myself from the room. Opening up the email, I saw a message from the detective working the case against Beverly.

To: Caston Black
From: Detective Alex Alverez
Date: July 9, 2013
Subject: Case 9131104

Mr. Black—
The case against Beverly Holden is moving along nicely. I would like to find some time to meet with you regarding some developments about your birth

mother. Please get back with me as soon as you can to discuss this.

Detective Alex Alverez

Almost walking into a door, I stopped in my tracks. My real mom, what would that have to do with anything?

Terrance walked down the hall carrying my overnight bag with another change of clothes in it. "Sir, is everything okay?"

I slid my phone back in my pocket and scrubbed my hands over my face. "Afternoon, Terrance. Just got a new email from Detective Alverez."

"Anything new that I need to be aware of?"

I looked up at the ceiling, thinking over the email. "I'm not sure yet. I'll let you know."

"Very well, sir. Is there anything else I can do for you?"

I shook my head and turned to walk back to Sabrina's room. Dr. Dana was just walking out of the room. She turned toward me when I approached.

"It went well. She seems to be resting comfortably. Her IVs are still in, but the breathing tube is gone. She looks more like herself. Now we wait to see if she will wake up. Her CAT scans have shown no brain damage, so we just keep playing the waiting game."

"Thank you, doctor. I'll never be able to show my appreciation for everything you've done for her."

"Well, we still aren't out of the woods yet, but we're getting closer to the light." Her smile touched her eyes, and I felt like she was confident that Sabrina would make it through.

"Mr. Black, this is good. She'll, hopefully, come back to us soon." Her hand on my arm was comforting.

I walked back into Sabrina's room, taking up residence in the chair right next to her bed. I grabbed her hand, as I have for the last few days, stroking my thumb over her soft skin. I silently willed her hand to grab it back, squeeze it—do anything. Even though I couldn't see her beautiful eyes, I knew we were still connected. I could feel it in my heart.

The only sound in the room was the beep of a heart monitor and the buzz of the iridescent lights.

I felt fingers twitch beneath my hand, causing me to jump unexpectedly.

"Sabrina?" My voice sounded rough.

Her heart rate sped up slightly on the monitor.

"Sabrina, honey, please open your eyes. Look at me."

My hand moved to brush the hair stuck to her forehead off. Why wouldn't she open her eyes? Fuck!

"Honey, please." My voice shook.

Then I felt it again—just barely. Her finger twitched.

"Honey, are you there? Bre, please open your eyes. I need to see your hazel gems." I pressed a soft kiss to her temple.

A loud beep sounded through the room. "Can I help you?"

"She moved. Please, send someone in."

"Right away, sir."

I grabbed both of her hands, willing her to wake. I felt like my heart was going to beat out of my chest with excitement. Suddenly, the monitors went wild; beeping, alarms going off. My stomach churned. *Oh God, what now?*

A rush of people entered the room. "Mr. Black, please, give us space. Why don't you step outside?"

"No! She moved, damn it, I felt it. Sabrina, show them!"

I felt multiple hands on me, trying to get me out of the room, but that just wasn't an option. I watched as someone even opened her eye lids, looking for some sort of reaction. Her bed was moved up and down, and she was shifted into a different positions. The monitors finally calmed. I took a deep breath and released a sigh of relief.

"She seems to be fine, I'm not sure why the monitors reacted the way they did. Her bandages look clean still. It had to have been her muscles twitching. I'm sorry, Mr. Black, but she doesn't seem to be coming out of this," Dr. Dana said.

The room was silent again. Beep, Beep, Beep, Buzz...

I wanted her here with me. *Please, come back to me, Sabrina.*

Bre and I were connected. Our souls were one. We were both fucked up and broken, but together we made each other whole again.

I couldn't stay away, I sat on the side of the bed, took her hand mine, and started stroking my thumb over her knuckles again. I wish I could hold her in my arms, pull her into me, and place a deep kiss on her tender lips. I wanted to feel her heart beat on my chest as I held her close to me, snuggled safe in our bed.

The door swung open, bringing me out of my thoughts. Jon walked in carrying food and a change of clothes. He set a stack of paperwork down on the windowsill and turned toward me.

"Caston, you need to go home, get some rest. You can't live by her side. The doctors aren't sure when, or if, she will wake up."

My head snapped up, and I stared him down. "Are you fucking kidding me right now? Can you honestly tell me that if this was Sara you'd leave her alone like this? Do you know she moved today?"

His eyes widened, and he moved closer to her bed. "I know, buddy, but maybe you just thought she did. I mean they said that muscles twitch and shit when people are in comas."

I shrugged off the hand he placed on my shoulder. "Don't pander to me, Jon. She moved."

14

"Shit, chill out, bro, fine—she moved. Go shower, you reek. I'll sit with her."

I sighed, looking back over at Bre. I stood and placed a kiss on her cheek before heading to the bathroom to clean up.

Before I shut the door, I saw Jon did in fact take up my vigil next to Bre. I heard him whisper, "Baby girl, you need to wake up. Caston isn't himself. Sara's a mess. I need the people I love to be happy again, and you seem to be the tape holding them together." He placed a kiss on her forehead, and, if I'm not mistaken, Jon sniffled.

Chapter Two

Sabrina

The smell of soap drifted through the air, tickling my senses. Caston must have taken a shower, I thought. Then I felt it, a warm sponge moving along up my leg and down the other, ever so slowly. I recognized the hands. Caston was bathing me. There was music playing in the background. It was too quiet to recognize, but it seemed to calm me.

I felt my eyes flutter, and my heart skipped a beat. Caston was facing away from me, taking care of washing my feet.

He was wearing a tight white t-shirt with worn blue jeans that fit him in all the right places. I felt butterflies in my stomach. He's here, my Caston is here. I love this man so much.

"Cass?" I whispered. My throat hurt and felt like it was on fire. I tried to move, but my arms and legs felt like lead.

Caston swung around so fast he knocked the pan of soapy water onto the floor. "Sabrina?"

I tried to smile. His arms were around me, pulling me into him, before I could even process moving. His kisses landed all over my face. "Sabrina, I knew you wouldn't give up. I just couldn't believe when they said you might not come back to me. I love you, Bre."

Tears started trailing down my cheeks. Just as his lips found mine, a crash of glass pulled us apart. Sara had just turned the corner into my room. She was stopped dead in her tracks, staring at me like she didn't believe what she was seeing. The floor was littered with broken glass, flowers, and the bag of food that she had brought for Caston. She rushed to the bed side and scooped up my hand in hers, tears falling down her face.

Nurses and doctors rushed into the room when they heard the commotion. Caston and Sara were moved away from me. I kept my eyes glued to Caston. His silver blue eyes had a red tint to them. How long has he been sitting by my side?

He smiled. His perfect lips mouthed, *'I love you, baby'*. I felt like everyone was moving in slow motion and they would never leave.

As I looked around the room, I couldn't believe the amount of flowers and cards lining the walls and window sills. Sara was by the windows on her phone. Finally, the last nurse and doctor left my room, and Caston was immediately by my side, his lips covering mine. I raised my hand to try to pull him closer to me, but I was stopped by the IVs. I backed out of the kiss and frowned. "How long have I been like this, Caston?"

His hand cupped my cheek, and I placed my hand over his. The warmth spread through my body. "Sabrina, it's been a little over a month. I was so scared."

My mouth fell open. "My dance review, graduation—the shooting and Beverly?" I felt my eyes start to water. My breathing became heavy and shallow.

"Professor Lee passed you without the review. She didn't need to see you dance."

"But, Caston, how will I get a job dancing, not being part of the review? That's all my parents ever wanted. All I've ever wanted." Tears threatened on their brink. Any minute they were going to fall.

Caston leaned forward and lightly kissed my forehead. "Bre... how can I tell you this?" He paused, looking sick.

"What?" I whispered, barely able to talk.

"The doctors aren't sure if you'll be able to dance again."

I pulled out of his embrace. "What?"

He swallowed hard. "I'm so sorry, Sabrina."

I laid back on the bed and faced away from him. I couldn't breathe. My life had been taken away, even though my body drew breath. One split second and everything changed. My chest hurt, as if someone squeezed my heart. I began sobbing uncontrollably. "My whole life I've wanted to be a dancer. My parents gave up so much for me to get where I was. They even gave up their lives, and now I can't even give them this one last thing."

"Your parents would be proud of you. For the women you've become. One thing I promise you, Sabrina, I will do everything possible to help you get back to dancing. I won't give up if you won't." He stroked my head, trying to calm me.

Caston walked to the other side of the bed and tipped my face toward his, making me look up at him. Brushing the tears away he looked deep into my eyes, whispering, "Sabrina, tell me—please, tell me what happened with your parents."

Shaking my head, I pulled away, looking at him terrified. "No, I can't—not right now. It's too much, too soon."

He took my head in his hands and rested his forehead on mine, kissing my nose before he placed a chaste kiss on my lips. Pulling back, he looked me in the eyes. His icy blues were a blaze. "When you're ready, baby. I'll be here to listen."

I choked on some tears. "Funny thing is that over the past year, I was tired of trying to make it. I was tired of dancing. I knew I wanted more from life, but I couldn't let my parents down. Not after all they gave up for me."

"Don't do this to yourself. Just get some rest. If you want to dance again, you will. I'll make sure of it. If you want to do something else, say the word. We'll get through this. I'm not saying it will be easy. Fuck, it's going to be harder than anything we've ever gone through, but together we can do anything."

Dr. Dana came in, interrupting us. I tried to listen as she explained exactly what happened and confirmed what Caston said about how I might not dance again.

Once we were alone again I look over at Caston. "It's going to be a long road, huh?"

He pulled me closer to his side and kissed the top of my head. "Yes, baby, a long road."

We sat in silence. I enjoyed his strong arm around me. Listening to his heartbeat, I felt myself drift to sleep on his chest.

Waking with a start, I realized Caston had fallen asleep on my hospital bed too. I smiled at him. He looked so uncomfortable, poor guy. I slid over further to give him more room. He must have sensed the room because he moved closer to the middle of the bed and rolled toward me. Turning the television off, the room fell into semi darkness. I slid down and rolled, as best as I could, to face him. I loved watching him sleep. I let my hands brush some of the hair off of his brow and followed the line of his face before placing a light kiss on his lips. He smiled and reached out hooking my waist, he pulled me to him. I immediately drifted back to sleep.

Nurse Kelsey woke us up the next day, informing us that we were being moved to another floor in the hospital, since I didn't need to be in ICU anymore. It was a private wing with restricted access. Caston had informed me that the press were camped outside, waiting for any information they could glean from anyone, and he had to ensure my safety. I was taken back that people were wondering about me.

Once we were settled into the new suite, I barely had a second to relax before my physical therapist entered the room, announcing it was time for me to start physical therapy. Caston helped me up and started to lead me to the wheelchair.

"No, sir, Dr. Dana has in her paperwork that Ms. Bennett has to walk to therapy."

We both stopped and looked at her.

"But, I can't put pressure on my leg. It hurts too badly."

She pulled out a walker and shrugged. "Orders are orders. Sorry."

I placed both hands on the cold plastic handles of the walker and shifted my weight to my good leg. Caston had his hands on my waist. Looking over my shoulder at him, I took my first step. The pain radiated through my leg. I whimpered and my eyes welled up with tears.

"She can't do this," Caston said a little more forcefully.

"Caston," I said in a warning tone, "if I don't, I'll never heal right."

He nodded, and I took another step with Lisa's help. We slowly made our way a few doors down to a PT room on the same wing. I bit my lip so much I was surprised it hadn't bled.

Out of breath and with tears about to spill, I pleaded, "Can I, please, sit down?"

I was relieved when Lisa nodded and helped me to a chair. Caston was right by my side with a Styrofoam cup of ice water. It felt wonderful going down my parched throat.

"Ten minutes. I'll be back, and we'll continue, okay?" Lisa said as she headed out the door.

"Can I get you anything?" Caston asked, kneeling by the chair.

"No, I'll be okay. One step at a time, right?"

"I love you. You're doing amazing, my strong girl."

Just as I was about to answer, Caston's phone rang.

"Caston," he answered with a scowl on his face. He stood and covered the phone. "Baby, I have to get this. Will you be okay?"

I grabbed his hand, squeezed, and smiled. "Yes. Go."

He bent over and captured my lips with his mouth. I was breathless again as he pulled away. Taking another sip of water to calm my burning insides, I watched as he walked out of the room.

Chapter Three

Caston

I saw on the caller ID it was Detective Alverez and scowled. He's the last person I wanted to talk to at the moment. Leaving Sabrina, I made it back down the hall to her room, shutting the door for privacy before speaking.

"What do you need, Detective? I'm kinda busy."

The background noise over the line was distracting. "Mr. Black, there has been a snag with the holding of Mrs. Holden."

My hands ball up into fists. "What!"

"I'm doing everything in my power to keep her locked up, but we might not be able to."

I punched the wall. "Are you fucking kidding me? Bre almost died, and that isn't enough to hold her! She shot her for God's sake!"

"I know, I'm so sor—"

"Don't fucking tell me you're sorry, FIX IT!"

I was so angry I hung up on him and threw my phone across the room. It hit the wall and broke into hundreds of pieces. *FUCK!*

Walking to the window, I looked out over the city continuing on below us as if nothing happened. It's just wasn't fair. I heard the door open and turned to see Terrance standing in the doorway.

"I need a new phone."

He nodded his head. "And?"

I crossed my arms over my chest and leaned back against the cold granite window sill. "They might be releasing Beverly. What a fucked up legal system we have."

Terrance reached for his phone and typed a message into it. Looking back up at me, he said, "Where do we go from here?"

I rubbed my forehead. "I don't fucking know."

Hearing Sabrina's voice out in the hall, I rushed over to the door, walking past Terrance. Stopping, I turned around. "Not a word about this in front of Sabrina. She isn't to know a thing until we have answers."

"Very well, sir."

Helping her back to her room, she was once again out of breath and exhausted. She sat on the edge of the bed and smiled. It lit up my soul.

"Is everything okay?" She questioned as she mindlessly massaged her leg.

"Nothing for you to concern yourself with. I just want you to focus on therapy and getting out of here."

A genuine smile crossed her face. "Me too, Caston. You have no idea."

I laughed and helped her swing her leg up onto the bed before getting her set up with lunch. She turned on the television. I quickly changed it from the news because they've still been reporting on what happened, and I wasn't ready for her to hear it through the eyes of the press.

After lunch she nodded off for a quick nap. Terrance arrived with my new phone, and I thanked him for his quickness.

In the afternoon, Bre and I were surprised when Lisa said that she has another PT session.

"Dr. Dana wants to kill me," she grunted. I had to suppress a chuckle.

Lisa just smiled and replied, "No, she just wants you back on your feet and out of here sooner rather than later."

The next few days continued on in the same manner. I was thankful to feel her arms around me at night, though. We shouldn't have been sharing a bed, but we couldn't go without holding each other any longer.

I was shocked with how quickly Sabrina had been healing and how steady she'd gotten in the first few days of therapy. About a week after her first session she flashed me a wicked smile, and I felt my cock twitch.

"Caston?" I was a goner. Her tone made me want to do anything she asked.

She slid to the edge of the bed and moved her legs over the side.

She gave me her best puppy dog eyes. "Cass, I think I'd feel better if I had a shower. Would you help me?"

"Sabrina, I don't think—"

"Please," she begged.

"You know I have no strength to say no to you," I answered as I caught her in my arms when she began to lose her balance as she stood too quickly. "Are you sure this is okay?"

She reached up and grabbed my face. Pulling me toward her, she passed her tongue over my lips. I opened slightly to give her access, and she deepened the kiss.

I felt her sway in my arms, and I was increasingly more concerned this might not be the best decision. "I think you're too weak to take a shower."

She bit her lip. It got me every time. "Your kisses always make me weak in the knees, so that doesn't count."

I sighed. "Maybe we could try. Come on, let's get you showered."

We walked slowly into the bathroom. "Maybe you could come in with me to make sure I'm safe?"

A cavernous groan rumbled deep in my throat, and my cock strained through my jeans. "Bre, you're killin' me."

She slowly shuffled alongside me as I led her to the shower. Once we reached it, I slowly lifted her shirt and lowered her pants. I couldn't help myself. My hands were on her back, taking in the feeling of her soft skin. Goosebumps pebbled at my touch. Her breath caught as I reached around and cupped her breasts. My fingers rolled her nipples into hard peaks. Fuck, I needed her so bad.

I moved her into the shower and got her seated on the bench. Reaching forward, I turned the water on and stepped to the side as the water washed over her. She sighed immediately, and I knew this was the right decision.

She looked over to me. "It feels like pounds of dirt are sliding off of me."

I laughed quietly.

"I guess, since I've been the one to give you sponge baths the last few weeks, I should help you shower too. It's only right." I flashed her the smile she could never refuse.

She held out her hand to me inviting me in, so I quickly discarded my clothing. Guiding me into the shower, she directed me in front of her. My cock stood at full attention. I felt bad for my reaction, but it had been so long. Smirking at me, she licked her lips and pulled my hips into her, taking my cock in her mouth until it hit the back of her throat. She relaxed and took me in further than I remembered.

"Fuck, Bre, your lips, your mouth."

She swirled her tongue around my tip, careful to keep her teeth covered she bobbed her head and ran a hand up and down my shaft. My muscles twitched with the sensation of her mouth, and I knew she tasted my salty pre-cum because she moaned. The rumble of it sent unworldly mumbles escaping my mouth. I let my head fall back and slid my hands into her hair.

She moaned again and this time my balls tightened. Without warning, hot spurts flowed from my cock and filled her mouth. She sucked me in and swallowed every last drop. Once my spasms subsided, I pulled her head back by her hair and leaned forward, taking her mouth with mine.

"Baby, that was amazing, but you didn't need too."

"I did need it. I want to feel normal. Thank you."

"I should be thanking you." I laughed, kneeling before her. I pushed her legs apart carefully. "Now, I'm going to return the favor."

Chapter Four

Caston

I hated leaving her, but Sabrina assured me she was fine and she would see me soon. Dr. Dana also said everything looked good, her muscle was healing nicely, and she should be able to come home soon and have PT on an outpatient basis.

Getting out of the car, I was bombarded with press asking me questions about what happened, if Sabrina was okay, what was going on with Beverly? I just slid on my sunglasses and pushed my way through without a word. Fucking vultures. It didn't matter what you told them they'd spin it the way it would sell the best.

Arriving at the doors of the court house I was greeted by my lawyer. He quickly fell into step with me.

"Any news?"

He scowled. "No."

I stopped, my shoes squeaked as I turned to face him. "Horse shit." I said a little too loud, causing people to stop what they were doing and look over at me. I poked him in the chest and seethed through my teeth, "She can't fucking get away with this."

He held up his hands. "I know, Mr. Black. We have all our people on it. I'm not sure why the judge called this meeting."

Turning to find the room, I saw Sara and Jon up ahead. Jon had his arm around her waist, pulling her into his side protectively. Reaching them, I bent over to kiss Sara on the cheek and slapped Jon on the back.

"Ready?" I huffed.

Sara looked up at me with sorrow in her eyes. "I'm so scared, Caston."

Jon pulled her into his embrace. "Honey, whatever happens we *will* be okay."

My lawyer shook hands with Jon and Sara's lawyer. I had wanted to use the same one, but they advised me it could be judged as a conflict of interest. He nodded to the guard once we were seated to indicate that we were all set. Thankfully, this was a closed hearing, so there was no press or extra people in the courtroom.

We all took our seats before they brought in the bitch.

I gritted my teeth when she walked in laughing and smiling with the guards. I wanted to jump over the table and beat the shit out of her, so I grabbed my legs and squeezed hard.

As she walked past us, she had the nerve to link arms with one of the guards and look over at us. "Hello, loves, Thanksgiving together? I'm willing to forgive and forget."

Before any of us can say anything, my lawyer held his hand up to us. I nearly bit my tongue off trying not to say anything.

"Mrs. Holden, no talking to them, remember?" The guard cooed.

She looked back to him. "Oh, silly me. I must have forgot. I'm so sorry."

"It's okay, ma'am, just, please, don't do it again."

The bastard actually blushed. What the fuck? She sure knew how to brainwash people.

I loosened my grip on my legs, and Sara reached for mine and Jon's hands. We all stood when the judge entered. The chairs creaked when we returned to our seats.

The judge shifted some papers around before looking up at each table. "Thank you all for joining us this afternoon. It has come to my attention that there has been some discrepancy with evidence. I had originally held Mrs. Holden without bail, but given the circumstances, I have to reverse my decision and grant bail. Bail is set at one million dollars."

"What!" I jumped out of my seat, Sara and my lawyer pulled me to sit again.

"Mr. Black, please, don't make me hold you in contempt. As I was saying, bail is set, let's set the trial for three months from today."

He got up and walked out. Just like that things were turned upside down again. How does she do this?

Jon consoled Sara as she started to cry, and I turned to Detective Alverez, who was seated behind us. "Fix this now. She shot her. For fuck's sake, what else could they need? We all saw her."

He ran his hand along his collar. "I'm working on it. She's going with self-defense and, well—"

"Don't." I stood up and moved to walk out, but my lawyer grabbed my arm.

"Remember, even though she's getting out, we have a standing restraining order against her to protect you, Sabrina, Jon, and Sara. That means no contact what so ever. If you go someplace where she already is, the law says she must leave, not you."

I nodded. "This is bull shit."

"I know. We're working on it."

I was too angry to talk to anyone right then. I headed out the back of the courthouse to try to avoid the press. If I'd gotten in front of a camera right then, it wouldn't have been good. Seeing that the coast was clear, I headed down the alley and out to the street on the opposite side of the block. I'd texted Terrance, telling him I was walking to the office. He immediately tried to call me, but I didn't want to hear it. I needed to clear my head.

Three months until the trial. Three fucking months to deal with her shit. I wouldn't let her get away with this. Over my dead body would that happen, she'd done enough to fuck with my life. I was in a zone, not paying attention to where I was going, and I knocked shoulders with someone.

"Watch it."

His voice sounded familiar, but not placing it, I mumbled, "Sorry." He was already a good six feet or so from me with a hoodie pull up, so I couldn't really see his face, only some blond hair sticking out from the hood and his hands were in his pockets.

I continued on to the office, once again I went in through the back door. Since it's isolated back there, I was able to make it to my office with very few employees seeing me.

No sooner did I sit at my desk, my phone vibrated in my pocket. Recognizing the number, I quickly answered.

"Bre, what's wrong?"

She laughed. "Nothing silly. Why do you always assume something is wrong when I call?"

I brought my computer to life and went through my emails, mindlessly seeing if there was anything that needed my attention immediately. "I'm sorry, babe, rough day."

"Oh?" I could hear the concern in her voice.

"Nothing for you to worry about, Bre. Just focus on getting better."

"Well, that's what I wanted to tell you." I could feel her smile through the phone. It was infectious. "They said I could go home today or tomorrow, depending when you got back. Please, tell me it'll be soon, I really don't want to be here anymore."

I was already out of the door, locking it behind me. "I'm on my way."

"See you in a few."

"Love you, Bre."

"Oh, Caston, I love you too."

I was sprinting down the hall and running out to the parking garage with Terrance hot on my heels, even though he wasn't sure what exactly was going on. He must have seen me on the security cameras.

"Sir, what is it?"

"Sabrina. We have to go now."

He unlocked the doors, and I climbed in. "What happened?"

There was a look of concern etched on his face. That's when I realized I didn't actually tell him. "She's coming home. They're releasing her."

Terrance relaxed immediately and smiled.

Chapter Five

Mark

I walked through the store and passed the tabloids. I saw *her* face plastered all over them. Some were with him and some were alone. I wanted to take every single one and throw them all over the fucking place. I wanted to stomp on her face. She didn't deserve a fucking happily ever after. I grabbed a few and tossed them in my basket. I felt like a fucking douche for buying them.

The giggly store clerk smiled, and I scowled. When the clerk came to the magazine, I saw her sigh.

I captured her wrist that held the magazine, and she gasped, locking eyes with me, I caught the look of fear, but I snaked a smile on my face. Grazing my thumb over the increased pulse on her wrist, my fucking dick was hard off of the fear in her eyes.

"When's your break?" I asked as I looked over the counter at the short fucking skirt she had on.

Her smile was devilish. "In about five minutes."

Smiling, I brought her hand up and kissed the wrist I was just hurting. "I'll meet you out back."

Grabbing my purchases, I headed to my car and threw my shit in the back. Getting in the car, I pulled around back and waited for her. Right on time she walked out, twirling her hair around her finger. I purposely parked where she couldn't see me. I needed to observe her for a few seconds. Palming my cock through my jeans, I watched as she lit up a cigarette and relaxed against the side of the building, letting her head rest on the cement wall.

I quickly got out of my car and stalked up to her before she even had a chance to react to my presence. In one swift move, I flicked the cigarette out of her mouth, covered it with one hand, and grasped her wrists together, binding them behind her back with my other, all before she was able to react. Putting my face directly next to hers, I whispered in her ear, "Don't fucking scream, don't make a fucking noise. Understand?"

Her big brown eyes locked with mine, and she nodded her head. Taking the hand away from her mouth, I lifted her skirt and drug my finger between her legs.

"You fucking like to be manhandled, don't you? You're so god damn wet."

Taking my cock from my pants, I managed to sheath myself with one hand. I ripped her thong off her body, throwing it to the ground

Thrusting my cock into her pussy was heaven. She was so wet. "Fuck, honey, you feel so good."

I slammed into her harder and harder.

She felt so warm and good. I felt my orgasm start to build. A few more pumps and my balls tightened to my body. The ripples flowed, and I came hard in the condom.

I pulled out of her body. Taking off the condom, I tied it shut and tucked myself into my pants. She straightened herself.

"Thanks, Mark. I needed that. I love when we pretend we don't know each other."

"Nina, you're ruining it."

She laughed and took out another cigarette. I pulled it from her lips and took a drag before handing it back. "Next time, I want you to suck my cock."

She made a clicking noise with her tongue. "Nope, you know I don't do that."

I leaned closer to her ear. "You will, and you'll enjoy it."

Pushing myself off the brick wall, I walked back to my Charger. Slamming the door, I started the car and pealed out of the lot, leaving two very long black tire marks.

Off to the courthouse to see what this judge was going to do.

Having to park a few blocks away, I took the back route. I saw him. He looked like he was in his own little world. Wanting to fuck with him, I pulled my hood over my head and moved so I would run right into him.

Clipping his shoulder hard, I muttered, "Watch it, buddy." I kept walking, wondering if he would recognize my voice. He didn't, and I just laughed. I must've been late, though, if he was already walking away from the courthouse. I quickened my speed, making my way to the jail that's attached to the courthouse.

The clock clicked over to three in the afternoon, and I shifted uncomfortably on the metal bench in the visiting room. The door buzzer sounded and the prisoners walked through in a single file line. Most of the people around me jumped up and hugged their loved ones; however, I stayed seated until she reached me. I kept my eyesight lowered. White tennis shoes came into my line of sight, and I stayed frozen.

"You may look at me."

A shiver traveled through my body from her words. I shifted my gaze up. She placed her hand in front of me. I accepted it and placed a soft kiss on the back.

"I've missed you, Mistress."

She slid in across from me and crinkled her nose. "You reek of sex."

I blushed and looked down at the table. "I'm sorry, Mistress."

"Shut up, Mark, you aren't fucking sorry."

I dared to look up at her. I saw the evil gleam in her eye. *God damn, I love her.*

She shook her head and looked away. "You disappoint me."

"Beverly, please—"

Her head snapped back around and her eyes darkened. "You are not allowed to call me Beverly."

"I'm sorry, Mistress."

Noticing the guards weren't looking, she leaned over the table and whispered in my ear, "If I was alone with you right now, I'd fucking whip you to a bloody pulp." She licked the outer edge of my ear before biting down on it hard. I whimpered, and my cock strained in my pants.

She leaned back and glared at me as she crossed her legs.

"I suppose you heard I'm up for bail?"

"No, ma'am."

She scowled. "You didn't make it to the hearing on time. I expected to be out already."

I hung my head. "I'm so sorry."

"Whatever, what news do you have for me?"

I looked around at all the happy families and frowned. "She's still in the hospital, but I have it on good authority that she will be getting out today, actually."

"Have they set a date yet?"

I shook my head. "Not to my knowledge. I'm sure they will soon."

"Well, their wedding will be a living nightmare that they won't survive." She laughed. That sound made me shiver, and my cock twitched.

"Am I making you hard, little boy?"

I nodded.

"If you bail me out, you can take me home, and I can have my way with you."

"I'd like that, Mistress."

Chapter Six

Sabrina

TWO MONTHS LATER—Present Day

My heart is beating a million miles a minute. I'm running as fast as my legs will take me, through alleys and down back roads I've never seen before. My chest is tight and the puffs of steam from my breath surround me in the cold. The dark shadow following me is making me run faster down the street. That's when I hear the bang. Pain radiates through my leg. I collapse to the ground. "Help," I scream, "please help me." Blood is everywhere. Reaching down I touch just above my knee, it feels like mush. I start shivering and crying. *Why is no one helping me?*

Sitting up in bed, I'm drenched in sweat and breathing hard. Tears are streaming down my cheeks. A warm hand reaches out to sweep my hair from my forehead. I gasp and jump as it touches me.

"Bre, it's okay," Caston soothes.

I take a deep cleansing breath as I try to shake the dream from my mind. "Oh, Caston, it was horrible. She was after me again."

"She can't get you, I promise."

"But she posted bail, she's out there somewhere."

He sits up and wraps his arms around me, I turn into his chest and breathe in his scent. Kissing him on the hard, solid muscle, I take comfort that I'm in our bed, in our home. It was just a few months ago I was lying in a hospital bed. Now my life consists of physical therapy every day, but at least it makes me leave the house.

He lifts my chin with his finger, making me look up into his ice blue eyes. "Bre, I promise."

"Are you sure?" Eyes wide from nerves.

He looks down at me and leans in to kiss my lips. As he captures them, he pushes a little, deepening the kiss and taking my breath away. In his husky, just awoken voice he assures me, "I swear on *my* life. Trust me."

"I trust you, Caston." My voice is barely audible.

Leaning down, slowly easing me onto my back, he starts kissing my jaw. I let out a soft moan as my insides clench with desire. His hands palm my breasts and tweak my nipples as his mouth sucks and nips its way down to the swell. Slowly his hands slide down my sides, he grabs the hem of my top and draws it up over my head. My long hair fans over my shoulders, framing my face.

"God, your beautiful, Sabrina," he says breathlessly.

His warm mouth sucks one of my nipples in, and his tongue twirls around, causing me to arch my back in pleasure. He starts trailing soft kisses down my stomach. His hands glide down my sides until he's gripping my hips as he presses his erection into my leg. I can feel how bad he wants me, and I've been craving him too. It's been way too long.

"I need you, babe."

As his fingers hook the tops of my silk panties, he tugs them down and brushes the scar on my leg. I immediately tense and pull away.

"I'm so sorry. Did I hurt you?" Worried, Caston sits up, looking down at me.

I quickly slip my camisole back on and inch away from him. "No, I just can't, Caston." A tear slips down my cheek, but I turn my head into the pillow before he sees me crying. My hand reaches down to touch my wrinkled skin above my knee, and my stomach churns, wanting to purge our beautiful dinner. It's so ugly and deformed.

"It's okay." He scoots in close to my back and pulls me into his embrace. Placing a kiss on my shoulder, he says, "I love you, Bre. I'm the luckiest man in the world. Do you know how beautiful you are?"

I take a deep breath in and silently blow it out. A few more tears slide down my cheeks, soaking my pillow. I can't respond when I don't feel those same things. I drift off, praying I can sleep peacefully.

Waking from another dream, my breathing is hard and shallow as my eyes flutter open.

Caston's hot body is still wrapped around me. I could tell by his even breathing that he was still asleep even though my body jolted awake. I move his arm off, gently sliding my body to the edge of the bed. Pausing briefly as I swing my legs over, I look back over my shoulder at the sleeping man who loves me unconditionally.

I feel my chest start to tighten, and I know a panic attack is coming on. Not wanting to break down in front of him again, I grab my crutches and get myself into the bathroom before I begin sobbing. Resting my back on the closed door, I slide down to the floor, hanging my head between my knees. I'm crying so hard I'm on the verge of hyperventilating. My heart hurts, and my whole body is tense.

I need to focus on the good. I need to remember back to happy times. Looking down at my engagement ring, I twirl it around my finger, and my chest slowly starts to relax. Love, our love, will get me through this. He's being so strong for me. I need to be strong for him. We've both been handed some big bombshells. Life has a funny way of doing that when you thought you had it all figured out. We both vowed to each other we won't give up, and I have to believe we'll make it through.

Picking myself up, I hobble over to the sinks. I splash some cold water on my face and look at the reflection in the mirror. It's amazing how someone can look normal on the outside when they're torn to pieces on the inside. From the waist up I'm like I always was, but now from the waist down I'm deformed. The bullet from Beverly's gun did a number on my leg, ripping it to shreds. The doctors don't think I'll be able to dance again. I can't accept that. Therapy has been going well. It's tedious, but I know it's the only way to actually help my leg. Shaking my head, I keep my head held high. I can't let this define me. Step by step I will get my abilities back.

Hobbling out to the balcony, I settle down on a lounge chair and raise my legs up onto the ottoman. The warm, clear night lets me breathe easily. Leaning my head back, I stare at the moon and fall asleep again.

I wake up to the sun warming my face. I have a soft knitted blanket placed over me, and I know that Caston has been up looking for me. This has become second nature lately. It's been two months since I was in the hospital and a little over three months since the shooting, but I still can't seem to shake the dreams that haunt my sleep and the panic attacks that plague my waking hours.

Stretching to wake my tight muscles, I glance over at the door to our room. Seeing it's open, I take a deep breath to steel myself before I face another day. The cleansing breath wakes my senses with the smell of the soap from Caston's shower wafting out on the morning breeze.

Snapping out of my day dream, I swipe away the tears falling down my cheeks. Damn these things never seem to quit. Not wanting Caston to see me crying, again, I get up. He'd placed my crutches next to me, since I left them in the bathroom. My doctor said I shouldn't use the crutches and I should actually work on using on my leg, but it still feels wrong and stiff. Plus, I get around a lot faster with them. Making my way through the room, I'm out the door and heading for the stairs before Caston comes out of the bathroom.

We only moved back up here a few weeks ago. We'd been staying in a spare room on the first floor, so I didn't have to climb the stairs with my crutches. It wasn't right, though. Yes, I was home and with Caston, but we weren't in our room, in our bed. Once my therapist assured Caston I could handle stairs with help, I convinced him to move back upstairs. Now, here I stand, regretting my decision. My stomach clenches.

As I'm about to take my first step down, I'm swept up into the arms of the man I love. I let out a small scream and playfully smack him on the chest. My crutches noisily tumble down ahead of us. "You scared the shit outta me."

He starts walking down the stairs, cradling me tightly. "I saw you staring at the stairs. You know you need help on these. So, I thought I'd be your knight in shining armor and rescue you."

He gives me a kiss on the cheek as he makes the descent.

"You smell wonderful," I tell him as I snuggle into his neck.

"Bre, I need you to stop that, or I will take advantage of you on the counter when we get to the kitchen, and I won't care that Jules is making breakfast."

It's been about a month since we've made love, and Caston has been extremely patient with me as I've come to terms with my injury. I remember the last time we had sex. It was after a business party that

Caston wanted to skip, but I insisted on attending, saying it would help me feel normal.

Caston and I were a little tipsy. I shouldn't have been drinking with the medicine I'm taking, but I snuck a few here and there without Cass seeing me. By the time the night was over, we were both giggling like idiots. We climbed into the back of the car, and as soon as Terrance pulled away, we were pawing at each other like teenagers. Never in my life have I been so brazen. I fucked Caston in the back of the car without caring who saw me. I don't even remember getting up to the bedroom that night. Waking up the next day, I felt like I was on my death bed. I told Caston I never wanted to drink again, and I couldn't look at Terrance for days after I was filled in on how we went at it in the car while he was driving. Not only did I feel like I was dying from the hangover, my leg hurt so badly Caston immediately took me to the doctor. Nothing was wrong, but she reminded us that we needed to take it easy. Ever since that day, I've tried to keep Caston at bay. It's been torturing me to turn him down.

"Earth to Sabrina," Caston whispers into my ear, bringing me back to him. A shiver travels through my body.

I look into his eyes. They're burning with lust. I cringe remembering how I left him last night. I try to pull away and move to have him put me down, but he holds me tighter. "Put me down, Caston. Please."

"Oh honey, don't do that. I didn't mean anything by it."

"I know. I'm just…" I wasn't sure what to say, so my voice trailed off.

Caston managed to pull out a chair before he set me down. As he slides into the chair next to me, I try changing the subject.

"I'm going to work today." I reach for the peanut butter. "I think it will be good for me to get out of the house for more than just PT, and I figure you'll be there, even if it is a different section."

"Do you really think that's a good idea, Bre? You don't have to go to work."

I gently set my knife down and fold my hands in my lap. Trying to mask my frustration, I say, "Caston, I will go crazy if I can't get out of here. Plus, Sara and Beth are taking me dress shopping today, so I won't be there the whole day." I look over at him and against my will my eyes fill with water again. "I need to get my mind off of everything."

He reaches for me and pulls me onto his lap. Brushing the hair off my face, he leans in and kisses my nose before resting his forehead on mine. "Sabrina, I won't hold you back. If you feel this is what you need, I won't stop you." Kissing my cheek, his lips slowly move to my mouth, nipping my bottom lip before parting my lips with his tongue. Our kiss is hungry, needy. My heart starts to beat faster as I feel his need for me growing against my ass.

His brushes the hair from my face again, and he reaches for my left hand, pulling it up to his mouth, he kisses it gently. I feel my engagement ring move beneath his lips, and my insides clench. God how I want to feel him inside me; it's been too long.

Chapter Seven

Sabrina

I excuse myself to head up to the bedroom with Jules's help to get ready for work. Pressing the power button on my iPad, "Feel This Moment" by Pitbull comes on. Perfect song, I think as I turn myself over to the music. Applying my makeup lightly and pulling my hair up in a loose bun on the top of my head, I head to the closet in search of something to wear. Letting my body take over, I sway to the music and do a few hip rolls, feeling sexy and like my old self. I pull out a lime green and black lace bra and matching thong. Sliding them on, I look over at myself in the full length mirror. For a few seconds, I see the old me looking back. I notice I'm bearing my weight on my leg and there's no pain. My heart warms, and I feel good. Turning around my leg gives out, and I'm brought back to reality as I catch myself on the dresser.

I close my eyes and give myself over to the music again, not wanting to think about what just happened. It's flowing through my veins, calming me. I touch my scar and mindlessly rub it as I reach into the drawer and pull out black stockings and a black garter belt. Sitting down on the bench in the closet, I pull the silk over my legs. Smoothing them as I get them positioned perfectly, straightening the line that goes from my heel up to the top of my thigh. Satisfied that the silk is just right, I slide my feet into my black pumps. I always felt sexy when I had my heels on. Standing up carefully, I turn to look at myself in the mirror once again. I smile when I notice the black stockings cover my hideous scar.

The song ends, and I stop in my tracks when I see Caston leaning on the doorframe of the closet with his arms crossed over his bare chest, his jeans resting low on his hips, and his bare feet. That man's body does delicious things to me. Meeting his eyes, I feel the heat melt me to my core. He scans my body starting at my heels. I feel them move slowly up as if he is touching me. My skin starts to tingle as he reaches my chest, and his tongue darts out, wetting his top lip. When his eyes once again lock with mine, my breath hitches and my heart speeds up. I see the outline of his arousal in his jeans, and my mouth starts to water.

Caston stands up straight and saunters over to me. His eyes never break eye contact until he reaches my side. Towering over me, I can feel the heat from his gaze radiating into my skin and a shiver goes up my spine. Letting the back of his hand glide ever so slowly down my ass cheek, it follows my curves to the top of my stocking on my left leg. He steps behind me, and his other hand snakes around my neck and turns my head to the side by my chin. I give myself over to him; closing my eyes as his mouth connects with the skin on my neck. The searing heat makes me moan, and I feel the dampness grow between my legs.

"You know I can't resist you in heels and stockings," he growls into my ear.

"Oh God, Caston."

I turn my head toward him, and his lips cover mine, quieting me. "Shhh…"

I whimper. His fingers trace over the hard pebbles of my nipples. My legs start to get shaky. Caston moves in front of me, reaching around my body. He cups my ass as his tongue dances with mine. We're both breathless when he finally pulls away, and I can feel how much he needs me.

"God I need you so bad." Pure animalistic lust flickers in his eyes when he says it.

I grab his head and pull his lips onto mine again as I grasp the hair on the nape of his neck. His growl in my mouth makes me whimper. He lifts me effortlessly, and I wrap my legs around his waist, letting him carry me to bed.

He sets me down and steps back slightly before he goes to his knees in front of me. "You smell wonderful, Sabrina."

I try to move his head to where I need relief, but he doesn't budge. Seconds feel like hours until I feel his finger slip under my thong, moving it to the side. He lets his finger slide up and down my hot pussy, spreading my wetness over my smooth folds. Slowly sinking two fingers into me, his thumb brushes my clit and sparks fly through my body. It's been so long since I've felt him, I'm about to lose my mind. I feel my orgasm hanging on the edge. His mouth slides down my body to join his fingers doing torturous things to me. His tongue makes contact with my swollen lips, sucking and nipping at them, lapping up my juices, and I'm thrown over the edge. Behind my eyelids stars and rainbows are shooting across my vision. I'm a convulsing mess as he strokes me down back to earth.

Slowly rising, he sinks the fingers that were once inside me into my mouth, and I suck them clean. My eyes connect with his, and I already feel myself panting, on the edge of another mind blowing release. He undoes the button of his jeans with his free hand and pushes them down past his hips, allowing his rigid cock to spring free into my waiting hands. I wrap them around his silky smooth length and spread the drip of pre-cum around his engorged tip. I'm torn between wanting him in my mouth and having him pound into me fast and hard.

Caston knows exactly what he wants as he removes his fingers from my mouth, he snaps the crotch of my thong and immediately rams into me hard and fast.

"You feel so good, baby—so good around me."

My nails dig into his shoulder blades and my head falls back, giving him better access to my neck and collarbone. He's sucking and nipping so hard I know there will be a mark, but I don't fucking care. It's been over a month, since I've had this man in me, and I need every sensation I can get right now.

I feel my muscles clench around his cock as my release shatters my mind. His teeth sink into my skin as his own release takes over.

"Holy shit! Caston, I love you so much!" I scream as another wave of ecstasy ripples over my body. Digging my heels into his ass, I pull him into me as close as he can get. I never want to let him go.

The sweaty sheen shinning on our bodies sends a shiver over my skin as we both come back to reality. I pull his head back by his hair and devour him. I can't even verbalize how I'm feeling right now. Feeling his cock twitch inside of me again, I separate our lips and smile at him, like a love sick puppy.

"Sabrina, I may not let you leave this room today." His smile turns devilish, and I feel myself clench in anticipation of all the sweet, dirty things we could do.

I take a deep breath and roll my head on my shoulders, bringing me back to reality. "That would be wonderful, Caston, but I really need to work, and I promised the girls we'd go dress shopping."

"Sabrina, it's been weeks. I need you. I need to feel you, hold you. Please, play hooky with me? We can get out of here. Let's go away. Where do you want to go? Caribbean, Hawaii, France? Just name it. Let's just go, you and me."

My stomach flips. It sounds so perfect and just what I need, but I look away from his pleading eyes, so I can keep my composure. "No, Caston. I can't."

He pulls out of me and adjusts himself back in his pants. I can see in his eyes he's hurt. Nodding he turns and walks out of the room, leaving me to collect myself in his absence.

Chapter Eight

Caston

Fuck! I want to hit something so damn hard. I just want to make love to my fiancée all damn day, escape reality with her, and I should be able to do that. She's so fucking sexy, but she doesn't see it. This injury has messed with her head. I hadn't had her in over a month, and today was heaven when I was able to sink into her. My cock starts to get hard again thinking about it. Damn body going against me. I throw on a t-shirt and shoes before leaving our room, slamming the door behind me.

I run down the stairs and head for the garage. Needing to get away as fast as I can to regain control of my temper, I don my helmet, and climb onto my Ducati 1199R. I want to get out of here, but I don't have a death wish. Safety first, no matter how upset I am.

Starting the bike I speed off, leaving a black mark from the rear tire in my garage. Turning onto the road, I try to clear my head and enjoy myself.

Finally having a clear head and my emotions in check, I decide to head into work. Sabrina should be here by now. We work on opposite sides of the building, but we usually cross paths during the day.

Pulling up to the front of Black Hollywood, I'm temporarily blinded by the camera flashes. Some of the paparazzi yell for me to look their way.

Taking off my helmet, I forgot how crazy it was in the front of the building. I'm used to pulling in under the cover of the garage. I set my helmet on the seat and walk into the building, greeting the employees as I make my way toward my office. Looking through some paperwork my secretary handed me I'm caught off guard when Lane, Black Hollywood's July Sweetheart and event planner, snuggles up to my side.

"Hey, Caston baby, I haven't talked to you in a super long time."

Trying to ignore her, I mumble, "Uh huh."

She steps in front of me, stopping me in my tracks and slides her arms around my neck. Her bottom lip protrudes out, and she whines, "Caston, I miss you. You aren't nearly as fun as you used to be, since shacking up with what's her name."

Before I even have a chance to react, she lunges up on her toes and places a kiss on my lips. I quickly grab her hands from behind my neck and push her off of me. Hearing someone gasp at the end of the hall, we both turn in the direction of the sound.

Sabrina stands frozen in her spot. Her mouth hangs open with unspoken words.

"Sabrina!" I yell for her.

My voice brings her out of her daze, she shakes her head and storms off around the corner out of sight.

Shoving Lane away a little harder. "Sabina is her name, and you know I'm off limits now, Lane. Fuck, what are you thinking?"

She keeps trying to get back to me. "Caston, we were so good together."

"Lane, you're done. Get your shit and leave. Don't ever step foot on BH property again. I will not tolerate your behavior."

Hastily getting away from her, I run down the hall. This was a huge mistake. Fuck what was wrong with me? I should have turned my head. I should have moved away as she came near me. Hell, I shouldn't have even come to the front door today, then I wouldn't have run into Lane. She was a plaything when I was single. Fuck, back in the day, I would've grabbed the bitch and took her into my office for a quickie. Not now, now I love Sabrina, she is my one and only.

I have to fix this! Taking off down the hall, I turn the corner and run right into Terrance.

"Sir, what's wrong?"

"Terrance, I fucked up. Please, make sure that Lane is escorted off BH property, tell HR I've let her go and get the paperwork for her termination started," I yell as I take off running down the hall to Sabrina's office and studio.

I pace back and forth in front of her closed office door and drag my hands through my hair. How would I even explain myself to her? She has every right to kick me to the fucking curb.

My text alert on my phone makes me jump as I fumble to get it out of my pocket.

Get the FUCK away from my office.

I hang my head as I type my response.

Bre, I'm sorry. I can't even explain to you.

Deleting what I just wrote I retype.

I'm sorry.

I wait by her door and listen to see if I hear any movement from inside. After what seems like hours, I push myself off the wall and shove my hands in my pockets as I dejectedly walk to my side of the building.

Entering my office, I slide into my seat and drop my head on the cold desk.

"Come in," I say when I hear a soft tap on the door. I don't even lift my head up because I know it isn't going to be Sabrina.

"Caston?" Sara says gently, "What's up?"

I groan. "I fucked up—bad."

I hear her walk closer to my desk, and I can smell her perfume. Lifting my head, I see the concern in her eyes. "Want to talk about it?"

Leaning back in my chair, I rest my hands behind my head and tell her everything that happened this morning to just now. She's very patient; never making a comment or interrupting me until I'm finished, even though I can tell she wants too. As if on cue the phone rings, and I motion to her to hold her thoughts.

"Caston Black—Terrance, thank you. I owe you one."

Turning back to Sara I tell her, "Terrance got all the paperwork done, so we won't be seeing anymore of Lane. He deserves a fucking raise."

"That's good to hear, Cass. Now what about Sabrina?"

Scrubbing my hands over my face, I think long and hard. "I have no idea, Sara."

My heart feels like it's busting into a million pieces, and I didn't know what to do to fix it.

"Well, you need to figure it out. Preferably before we go shopping today. She won't want to shop for a wedding dress if she's mad at you." Chuckling at her comment she ruffles my hair a bit.

"Hey, quit that." Trying to smile, I mumble, "Thanks for listening to me ramble."

She walks over to me, hugging me from behind. "Anytime."

I squeeze her arms that are around my neck. Clicking open my email, I immediately select the one from Detective Alverez and start scanning the contents.

"What's wrong?" she says. "You just tensed up."

"Detective Alverez thinks he found my real mom."

"What!"

I jump at the tone of her response. "He says he was looking into old records of Beverly's and came across something that didn't seem right. He wants me to call him."

She moves to the edge of my desk and rests on it, crossing her arms over her chest. "Are you going to?" I can see the concern on her face.

"I don't know. I need to talk to Sabrina." I cringe as soon as I say it. How can I talk to her about it if she isn't talking to me?

Sara looks down at her watch. "Well, she should be finishing up a shoot now and be heading back to her office. Then we're going dress shopping, so if I were you I would get to it, stud."

Leaning my elbows on my desk, I rest my head in my hands as my fingers run through my hair. I'll go bald before my time from stress the way I've been pulling at it the last few weeks.

Sara pats me on the back and leaves me to ponder what I need to do.

I push my chair away from my desk and head to the door. As I turn the corner, I nearly run Sabrina over.

"Jesus Christ, Caston!" Sabrina catches herself on the wall.

I grab her by the shoulders, trying to help. "Sabrina, I'm—Are you okay?"

"Fine," she snipes back at me. Rolling her shoulders and getting herself back on her crutches, she says flatly, "I just wanted to tell you that I'll be leaving soon to go with the girls. I don't know what time I'll be back. Maybe I'll end up staying at Beth's. I'm not sure."

"Bre, no," I say, dragging my hand through my hair again. *I have to stop doing that.* "Please, come in and sit down. Let me explain."

She backs up shaking her head. "I'd rather not, Caston. I think I saw enough this morning. If I feel like talking tonight, we might."

My heart sinks. If? "Bre, can I at least talk to you about something Detective Alverez emailed me about?"

Seeing her suddenly tense in front of me, I continue while shaking my hands in front of me, "Nothing about Beverly. We're still safe."

She puts a hand over her heart and takes a deep breath. I hate that I've put her through so much. That my past has caused her so much anguish in her life.

"Please, come in?" I entreat, holding my hand out to her.

She hesitates for a moment before snubbing my hand and hobbling into my office. I release the breath I didn't know I was holding. At least she was giving me this. *Tread lightly*, I told myself.

As she passes me, I take a deep breath—lilacs and Sabrina. My most favorite scent in the world. I follow her in, shutting the door behind me and locking it, ensuring we won't be interrupted.

I turn around and drink in the sight of my beautiful girl in front of me. Her brunette hair is still swept up on the top of her head in a messy bun. The tendrils that fall frame her face. She has a slight blush from the exertion of moving about on her crutches. Her lips are plump, and I want nothing more than to kiss them. She has a lime green camisole on that I know matches her undergarments. I feel my dick twitch at that thought. Her black pencil skirt stops right above the knee, hiding the scar and more importantly the tops of her black stockings and garter belt straps. I find myself taking a deep breath and swallowing hard, trying to keep myself from jumping her right here in my office.

"Caston?" she says, sounding annoyed.

"Sorry, please, sit," I apologize, shaking my head, bringing myself out of my daydream while motioning to the couch on the side of my office.

She props the crutches on my desk and walks slowly to the black leather couch. Seeing her walk on her own puts a smile on my face.

"I love that."

Quickly snapping her head in my direction she looks at me like I've got two heads. "What?"

"I love that you're walking there without your crutches. You seem to be getting steadier every day, baby. The doctor said you don't have to use them anymore. I'm not sure why you still do."

I see her clench her jaw. "I do what's best for me, Caston. Is this what you want to talk to me about, because if it is I'll turn right around and walk back out of here?"

"No, no," I say as I walk past her and wait to see where she'll sit.

Finally she sits on the couch. I move to sit next to her. I'm disappointed when I feel her tense under my touch and pull away, setting her hands in her lap while turning her head.

Not wanting to make anything more awkward than it already is I start, "Bre, I got an email from Detective Alverez saying he thinks he found my real mom and that she's alive."

Her head snaps in my direction, eyes wide as saucers, and her hand flies to her mouth, covering the escaping gasp. "What?" The sound is barely audible.

I hang my head and think about that email. "He has emailed me a few times, but I haven't responded yet. I'm not sure how to." I look up and lock eyes with her. "I'm not sure I want to."

"Oh, Caston." She moves closer to me, resting her hand on my leg, sending an electric jolt through my body. I love that her touch does that to me.

"Honey, you have to at least talk to him. See what he has to say. Trust me, if you don't, you'll never forget it and wonder what if. Caston," she places a hand on my cheek, "it's okay to be afraid. I can go with you if you want? You don't have to do it alone. Trust me, though, you will want to know. I'd give anything to have my parents back."

I slide a hand into her hair, and she leans into my hand. "Bre, will you tell me about how you lost your parents?"

Her eyes immediately well up. I feel bad asking, but I have to know her account of the accident. I've read the reports a million times. I don't see how she thinks it was her fault they died. It was a freak accident. Her dad lost control of the car in the rain.

Taking a deep breath she starts, "Dancing was my life. Ever since I was three, I'd been in some sort of dance class. My parents gave me every opportunity to make my dreams come true. They gave up so much, and I never thanked them. The house went into disrepair, they got second jobs, and carted me around at all hours just to give me the leading edge. Countless times I'd ask to take another class or to attend a special convention, and my parents never said no. I saw the worry lines grow deeper around my dad's eyes and the way he would look at their checkbook every month. There wasn't enough money to pay all the bills every month. But did they ever tell me I couldn't dance? No. I took advantage of being an only child. Every spare cent and more went to me and my dreams."

I pull Bre closer to my side, trying to calm her. I can tell that she needs my strength to get through this story.

"Caston, my parents lost their lives because of me."

Shaking my head, I run my thumb along her jaw. "I'm sure that's not true, Bre."

"It is, Cass." Tears start streaming down her face. I lean in to kiss them away, but she withdraws from my embrace, getting up to pace the room.

"It was my senior year of high school. I lived at school or the studio. Only four weeks before graduation, I had a rare night off. However, I begged my parents to take me to the studio on the way to the store, so I could get in a few extra classes. They hesitated, knowing extra classes meant more money, but like I said earlier, they never said no to me. Me and my selfish ways. We all should've been home eating dinner together, catching up with one another, but no, I insisted they take me to the studio. We got to the hill just before the studio, and it started to rain. When they dropped me off, I ran into the studio, never looking back at them when they drove away."

She stops walking and hides her face in her hands, sobbing into them. I immediately walked over to her, wrapping her in my arms. Holding her for a while before her tears slow. Lifting her chin to look up at me, I wipe her puffy eyes. Helping her back to the couch, I draw her onto my lap. She immediately curls into my neck before taking a shuddering breath to calm herself down.

Finally, she goes on, "It was about forty-five minutes before they were supposed to pick me up when there was commotion outside of the dance room. The teacher stopped class and went to investigate. When she came back in, she looked like she'd seen a ghost. She came over to me, taking me in her arms before she broke down crying. I had no idea what was going on, but my stomach started churning when I saw the police officers in the door way. My legs gave out from under me and my teacher and I sunk to the floor. I knew they were gone. They were gone, and I never said goodbye or that I loved them. I just ran off into the studio. Caston, I never even looked back. How could I have been so horrible? They should still be alive."

I tighten my arms around her. Lightly stroking her back, I kiss the top of her head repeatedly. My poor girl for keeping this in for so long. I wonder if she ever talked to anyone about that night before now.

"The rain made them lose control. They spun into oncoming traffic and into the path of a semi. They died immediately. I have no family, Caston. My parents were only children, and so was I. My grandparents are dead, so I was immediately an orphan. My teacher talked with the cops and social services. She took me in until I graduated. From that moment on, I spent every waking moment trying to become a professional dancer, so all my parents' hard work wouldn't go to waste. I almost lost my will to go on when I was with Mark, but since I've been with you my life has turned around. I thought I could finally make it for them."

"And you will, Bre. They're still with you. Every time you do something amazing in life, they're smiling down on you."

She doesn't respond. We sit in silence for a while. I'm thankful she finally told me and that I'm able to hold her close, offering her comfort. I want her to know I'll always be there for her.

I suck in a deep breath to calm my nerves. "Sabrina, I'm sorry about this morning,"

"Caston, shut the fuck up and…"

Our mouths collide in a needy, hasty kiss.

"Cass," she whispers.

"Hum?"

I lean in and place a kiss behind her ear.

"I'm not upset about that kiss this morning." She leans back and looks me in the eyes. "I know she caught you by surprise and you pushed her off of you after I turned around."

"But…"

"Don't get me wrong, I was livid when I stormed off. I couldn't believe you would do such a thing to me, but when I was talking with Sara, she told me you had pushed the skank off. What I'm upset about is you leaving me this morning when I told you I didn't want to stay in. It isn't that I don't want to, babe, I want to spend every waking moment with you, but I need to get back to some sort of normalcy. I had shopping planned and, well…"

I kissed her lips lightly. "I shouldn't have left. I was being an ass. You've been cooped up for so long that you need this outing with the girls. Plus, I don't plan on letting you out of our room on our honeymoon."

She took my head in my hands and turned me to look at her. "Now that sounds tempting."

Pulling me close, she nips my bottom lip before leaning in to deepen the kiss. Sighing into my mouth, she pulls away again. I groan at the loss, and she chuckles.

"It's still hard for me to get past this." She points toward her leg. "After you left this morning, it made me realize this thing isn't only hurting me and my mental health, but it's hurting you—us. That's something I don't want. I'm going to work on embracing it and moving forward."

That's the best thing I've heard her say in a long time. Tears begin to fall down her cheeks. I wrap my arms around her and pull her head down to rest on my chest.

Beginning to feel calm again, I stroke her hair and kiss her forehead.

She shifts to look at me and quietly asks, "Cass, why are you questioning meeting your mom?"

My heart begins to beat erratically. Withdrawing from our embrace, I set her to my side. Quickly getting up, it's my turn to pace the room.

Chapter Nine

Caston

Sabrina stands up and walks over to me. Wrapping her arms around me, she snuggles into my back. My breath calms immediately. I move her to stand in front of me. Cradling her to my chest, I kiss the top of her head. My heart hurts, it's so full of love for her.

"Bre, I need to talk to my dad about Rose before I talk to Detective Alverez. I want to hear it from him. I'm guessing he knows more than he's let on. I guess, I just don't understand why she—they—would keep it from me."

She looked up at me, her hazel eyes sparkled. "Okay, Caston, maybe you should have a guys' night with Jon and your dad to talk it over."

"That sounds like a good plan. Thank you."

I kiss her again, never getting enough of her.

"How soon are you leaving?" I manage to ask between our kisses.

She steps back quickly. "Oh my God, now!" Her voice is full of life, and I know, even though she doesn't want to admit it, she's excited to plan our wedding.

I kiss her nose and stroke my thumb over her cheek. "Go, have fun, but we will pick this up tonight when you get home."

The blush that creeps up her neck is a beautiful shade. I love that color.

I reach down and give her ass a swift smack. "Get going before you're late. Guys' night sounds like a fantastic idea, I'll set it up now."

"Smack my ass again and I might not want to leave this office," she growls into my ear, making my cock twitch.

Reaching my hands down her backside until I have them fully over her behind, I grab and pull her toward me. She slides her arms around my neck, grabbing on to my hair, and we lean into each other again.

A knock on the door separates us from our primal kiss. I walk over and open it.

"Did I interrupt?" Sara says as she wiggles her eyebrows, looking at me and then over my shoulder at Sabrina.

Sabrina slowly walks up behind me and wraps her arm around my waist as she slips into the crook of my arm.

"It's good to see you both happy again."

Kissing Bre on the top of her head, I squeeze her shoulder.

"I give Sabrina permission to spend all of our money today, but she won't do it, so I'm leaving that to you and Beth." I say to Sara.

"Caston," Sabrina tries to protest.

I quiet her with a kiss.

Sara starts squirming in front of us. "Damn it, you two, stop it, or I will join in."

Sabrina blushes. I know she's just as excited about that option as Sara is.

"Go," I whisper into Bre's ear, "I'll worship your body tonight."

She heads off down the hall with Sara, and I have to smile because she didn't grab her crutches.

Taking out my cell phone, I dial my dad.

"Hey, Dad… I'm good. I need to talk to you about something. Can you come over tonight for dinner and a beer? Okay, great. See you then."

Hanging up, I call Terrance to tell him I'm heading home, and then I make my way to the garage. Thankfully, Terrance had moved the bike after I got in, so I didn't have to go deal with the paparazzi again.

A few hours have passed, and I'm sitting on my couch mindlessly flipping through the channels while waiting on my dad to show up. I'm already tense and unsure how this is going to go. The weather outside has dimmed, there's a storm on the horizon.

Hearing the front door open, I mute the television and reach for my rum and Coke.

"Hey, son. How's it going?"

He walks over to the bar in the corner and pours himself something.

"Where's Jon? I thought he was coming."

"Nope." I said as I take another drink.

"Something the matter, son?"

I look over at him slowly. Taking another drink, I size up how this is going to go. Terrance is already stalking back and forth in the other room, I can see him out of the corner of my eye.

"You could say that."

He still doesn't have a clue that I'm upset with him.

"Something wrong with BH? Please, tell me it's not with Sabrina?"

I get up and walk to refill my drink. Turning around I rest my back on the bar. "So, Dad, tell me about my mom, Rose."

He immediately tenses, but he shakes it off. He smiles at me, "What do you want to know, Cass?"

"How about how she died."

"Caston, I've told you this all before. She was on her way home from work. It was dark and rainy. A car was speeding down the road and hydroplaned. It lost control and jumped the curb hitting her. Thankfully she didn't suffer because she died immediately. I paid for her burial. It was a just her and me, very intimate." He takes a huge gulp of his drink.

"Bull shit, James…"

His head snaps toward me. "Don't talk to me like that."

Glaring at him I walk over toward the couch. "But it is, isn't it."

"What are you talking about?"

"I think you know exactly what I'm talking about, Dad."

His mouth drops open, and he blinks a few times.

"How… what do you know?"

"I know she's alive. I have a meeting with Detective Alverez tomorrow to find out more, but I'd like to hear it from you."

He takes a deep breath and stares at me as if he was lost in his thoughts.

"I want the truth, don't fucking try to come up with some lie. I think you owe me this." I slam the glass down on the table in front of him, making him jump back.

"Okay. Caston, sit, please."

I back up and sit in the chair. Leaning forward, I rest my elbows on my knees and wring my hands over and over.

James backs up on the couch and takes a drink. It was slow and painful waiting for him to continue. Right now I didn't even want to call him Dad. Who lies to their son their whole life? Fuck, he would leave me with Beverly for days on end even though he knew she was crazy.

"Your mom is still alive," he says quietly.

"No shit, Dad… Tell me something I don't know."

"God, Caston, I am not sure where to start. This has been killing me, since the day I told you she was dead."

"Really, James?" I get up in his face and grab his shirt, "Fucking start at the beginning."

Terrance appears in the doorway behind my dad. He's tense, not sure how I'm going to react. Crossing his arms over his chest, he watches me closely. Knowing he's going to be there to back me up, I loosen my grip and shove James back onto the couch. I sit back on the chair and go back to wringing my hands.

A bead of sweat appears on his brow, and he puts a finger in his shirt pulling it away from his neck as if it is choking him.

"Okay, Caston. Please, settle down. Just let me start off by saying I—we—never meant to hurt you. We were only trying to protect you."

"Let me fucking decide that."

"Okay, okay." He holds his hands out if front of him to try to calm me. "You know your mom and I had an affair before you were conceived. Beverly never knew, or so we thought. I was days away from filing for divorce. That was the night we had the party and she pulled me into the room for a threesome. I froze when I saw the third was Rose. She looked surprised herself. I wasn't sure what to do with both of them together in the same room. I mean Rose was Beverly's sister, so we've been in the same room, but never for this type of situation. I tried to play it off the best I could, focusing most on Beverly, so she wouldn't be wiser. Afterward Beverly fell asleep, Rose moved over to my side of the bed she was panic-stricken. She was crying about how she had gotten a note from me to meet in my bedroom, but to come in the back door because there would be a party. She said that she never questioned it until Beverly had walked in with me. I tried to soothe her, telling her everything would be okay, but I didn't understand how this happened. I didn't send her a note."

He paused. Agitated I want him to continue. Slamming my hands down on the table besides me. "I know this shit already! Damn it, James…"

He started talking quickly now. "Beverly woke up and smacked Rose off the bed, hitting her multiple times before I pulled Beverly off of Rose. Beverly freaked the fuck out, spouting all this shit she had on me and Rose and how she would ruin us. I was terrified for Rose. Beverly was crazed, I'd never seen her this bad before. Rose was so scared on the floor, cowering in the corner. Beverly and I had it out, screaming, yelling, and hitting. Rose suddenly started getting sick and bleeding. Terrified I scooped her up, leaving Beverly without looking back. I rushed her to the hospital. I stayed by her side the entire time. That's when we found out about you."

"But, you told me you never knew about me." I whispered.

"I know, Cass, I'm so sorry."

"Whatever." I look away from him.

"You were just a little bean." He reached forward to try to touch my leg.

"Don't fucking touch me."

He pauses. "I decided that moment that I was going to leave Beverly. Getting Rose settled into the hospital for overnight observation, I headed home to finish the deal. When I got there Beverly was sitting on the floor in the bedroom with Jon in her lap. Thankfully he was sleeping, but she was rocking him with a butcher knife in her other hand. A fucking butcher knife! The look in her eye was ruthless, she told me every little dirty detail she had on me, all the blackmail she would ruin me with. I panicked. I'm so sorry, Caston. I couldn't let my business and everything I worked so hard for go to shit. Plus, she was the one that had the money to begin with. She funded my ventures. I had to do what she said. Not to mention she had a fucking knife threatening Jon."

He shakes his head and rubs his forehead. "I got her calmed down and vowed that I wouldn't leave her. I had to lay low for a week or so. I wanted to make sure Beverly believed me. When I went back to Rose, she was missing. I was frantic and went to her house looking for her. Her house was empty, like she was never there. They said she'd moved out. No forwarding address, no contact information. Her phone number was disconnected. I looked for her for years. I begged Beverly to give me her contact, I just knew she had something to do with her disappearance, but she always played the innocent. I just wanted to know about you, and I was worried about Rose."

Looking over at me he had the saddest eyes, but I wasn't falling for it.

"Four years later, Beverly handed me an address. I wasn't sure what it was, it was in the bad part of the city. I had all but given up until Beverly handed me that paper. Beverly told me I should go to that address today. My heart was in my throat when I walked up to that door. I was shocked when I got there. She was living in poverty. There was no food. She was crying. Rose hid you from me that whole time. I was furious with her. That's when I took you, brought you home to live with me, Jon, and Beverly. At the time I couldn't understand why Rose wouldn't try to contact me for help. Beverly took you right in and said that she was so happy to have another son, and she'd love you as her own. I fell for her lies… again."

I look into his eyes. "You fucking left her."

Snapping his head back up to me he glares at me. "Would you fucking let me finish? You are the one to who wanted to know."

We stare at each other for a few minutes in silence. His chest was rising and falling quickly.

Chapter Ten

Sabrina

Walking out of Caston's office I was in shock. His mom is alive? How? My thoughts consumed me. It wasn't until we got to Sara's car that I realize I'd walked the entire way without my crutches. I stop abruptly, causing Sara to almost run into the back of me.

"What the…"

I spun around, coming face to face with her. "I just walked this entire way without my crutches. I don't even feel tired and my leg doesn't hurt."

A huge smile engulfs her face. "I was waiting for you to notice."

I want to jump up and down, but I know better than to push my luck.

"You were a walking zombie. Apparently you made up with Caston, so what's on your mind now?"

Arriving at the car, I slid into the passenger side of her red BMW X6. "Caston just told me his real mom is alive. What do you know about her?"

She starts the car and turns to face me. "I know. He mentioned something to me. It's fucked up, but I only know what you do. I mean, he's told me the story James has told him, which I assume is what he's told you."

I nod, feeling slightly hurt she knew before I did.

"Caston will figure this out, don't worry." She pats me on the leg high enough to make my insides flutter.

Blushing, I look out the window. She laughs. "I love when you blush."

"Caston says the same thing all the time."

"I always knew he had good taste."

We both laugh. She backs out of her space and heads for the exit.

Driving in silence for a little while staring at the passing scenery I catch site of a blacked out SUV following us. My heart starts to beat hard when I notice it's doing exactly what we are.

"Get out of here, Sara. I mean now, let's go."

She looks at me confused, but floors it, weaving in and out of traffic. I keep glancing behind us as the black vehicle does the same, following our every move.

"What the fuck is wrong, Bre?"

"I think we're being followed."

Sara weaves in and out of traffic. I keep my eyes glued to the cars behind us. I see the blacked out SUV turn a few streets back. I take a deep breath and turn in my seat to face forward.

"They turned."

Sara quickly turns off onto a side street and throws the car in park. "Sabrina, my God, we could've been killed, the way I was driving. It was probably some random person driving down the street."

I cringe, feeling bad for scaring her. Sara's trying to catch her breath.

"I'm sorry, Sara. I could've sworn—whatever, it's over with, let's go pick up Beth."

She turns toward me and glares, her eyes shooting daggers. "Sabrina, you tell me someone is following us and now you say forget about it. No way. Spill it."

I bite the tip of my thumb and look out the window. The tension in the car could be cut with a knife.

"Sabrina." There's warning in her voice.

Turning back toward her I take a deep breath and start, reluctantly. "Okay, fine. The last week, or so, I've felt that someone has been following me, watching me. I'm just anxious. Caston hasn't noticed it, so I'm sure it's all in my head. I mean, this is my first day out without him. He would've noticed, wouldn't he?" My voice cracks with uncertainty.

"I didn't notice anything, Bre." She reaches across the car and touches my arm lightly, making me jump.

Shaking my head, I bite my lip. My voice starts to waver, "When we pulled out into traffic it did the same. Sara, I think I'm going crazy."

"Bre, you were stalked and shot. You're entitled to feel scared and unsure. This is your first time out without Caston, you're going to see things that aren't there. It's okay."

"Are you sure? How are you holding it together so well? You were kidnapped and held against your will too."

She nodded. "Jon and I turned it into a sex game. Made it a fucking hot fantasy." She blushes and shifts in her seat. "Yes, it's sick and twisted, but I guess that's who we are." She laughs, throwing her head back before looking at me seriously. "Yes, I'm also sure it's okay to be jumpy and unsure too."

She pushes a hair off my forehead, tucking it behind my ear. My insides warm. Forcing myself to smile at her, I didn't feel much better, but I put on a brave face.

"I do think you should mention it to Caston. I know you don't want to because he'll tighten your already short leash, but if there's someone following you and you didn't tell him..." She whistles shaking her head.

I laugh without humor. "You're right."

Sara starts the car and pulls out into traffic again. "I know I'm right. Now if you see the scary black vehicle again, can you tell me calmly?"

I smack her arm, and we both start laughing. "You're an ass."

"Oh, I like ass." She wiggles her eyebrows.

"Sara, you are something else." I roll my eyes.

She looks over at me and winks. "Would you want me any other way?"

Reaching over she grabs my hand and gives it a squeeze.

"No way," I say.

Traveling along in silence for a while, I think about the last few months and how my life has changed. What a whirlwind. Finally arriving at Beth's apartment, I smile at the memories we shared in her small living room.

"Ready to get your shopping on?" Sara asks as she parks the car in the guest parking spot.

"No," I groan. Shopping is a thorn in my side.

Turning toward me, she clutches her chest, like I'm giving her a heart attack. Just as I'm about to respond to her, there is a knock on my window. I let out a screech. Beth starts laughing hysterically as she jumps into the backseat.

"Who's ready to shop?" Beth beams.

Sara responds with a shriek, clapping her hands like a little kid. I turn to face the window, rolling my eyes at both of them.

They were gabbing back and forth about what style of dress I'd look good in and what color bridesmaid dresses they were going to look at. I take out my phone and send a text off to Caston as I tune out the chatter.

I miss you. Wish I was with you instead of here.

I palm my phone and gaze out the window again. All the talk of A-line, ball gown, and mermaid style makes me want to crawl under a rock. My phone chimes a return message.

I'll take care of you tonight. Just enjoy yourself. Love you.

I squeeze my thighs together, wondering what he has in store, idly pondering if he would consider going to the club tonight. Smiling at the possibility, I reluctantly give myself over to my girls and shopping.

"Earth to Bre…"

My head flips around to see Beth leaning over to the front seat staring at me, and I realize they aren't talking anymore.

"My God, Sara, look at the shade of red her cheeks are. What'd that text say?" She moves to grab my phone, but I pull it away just in time, before I shove it into my purse.

"Nothing. Just promises."

The girls giggle, and I see Sara eyeing me over Beth's shoulder. Pulling up to the shop, we all get out of the car. Sara has gone ahead of us to tell the consultant we're here for our appointment while Beth and I take our time. Beth gives me the biggest hug. "I've missed you girlie."

"Me too, Beth." I really did.

She links her arm in mine. "He treating you right?"

I stop short almost making her stumble. I look at Beth like she has two heads. "Are you serious? No offense, but I'd rather be with him then with you girls. If you know what I mean."

She laughs with me. "Great to hear, Bre. You deserve it. I'm so happy for you."

Wanting to catch up with her a bit, I ask, "Have you heard from Broc?"

She runs her hand through her hair and shakes her head. "He keeps trying to get me back. I use him here or there, when I need to get off, but that's about all he's good for. He needs to learn I won't always be there when he needs me. I know he still feels guilty for what happened to you."

I shrug my shoulders. "Beth, I never... maybe I should call him. I need him to know it was my fault, not his."

"He'd like to hear from you." Her face looks a little sadder. "I'd like to meet my prince charming, like you have."

It makes my heart hurt for her. I make a mental note to call Broc. Wrapping her in my arms, I whisper in her ear, "Beth, you deserve the best. You'll find the one, I can feel it in my bones."

We get to the door, and I take a deep breath. "Here we go..."

As we step through the open door, Sara turns around to look at us. She walks up to us, handing each of us a glass of champagne. "Who's ready to get this party started?"

Beth shrieks, and I groan. Sara laughs at me. Raising the glass, I down it in one gulp. I walk further into the room filled with white gowns. We wait for the consultant to meet with us to discuss what 'I see myself in'. The girls have their own ideas.

I reach for the champagne and fill another round. I sit quietly, trying to decide when I'll be able to get a word in, but since it looks like that isn't possible, I stand up and turn toward them.

"Okay, look, here are the rules; no crazy, expensive, over the top, cupcake looking dress. Got it? I have a budget in mind, and I'm sticking to it. I know Caston said it doesn't matter, but it matters to me." I point to Sara and then to Beth. "Got it?"

They laugh. "Got it. Maybe. If the dress if phenomenal you're getting it," Sara declares.

Shaking my head, I take another sip. "Now, on to the next important issue. I need my best girls at my side. I want Sara to be my Matron of Honor and Beth to be my Maid of Honor. Will you girls stand by my side and help me?"

They both jump up, almost tackling me, yelling variations of, oh my God, oh my God and yes! It was almost in unison.

The consultant finally joins us. We start going over styles, and I once again zone out, letting Sara and Beth work their magic.

Then the question of the hour, the consultant turns to me. "So, Sabrina, when is the wedding?"

They all fall quiet, waiting for my answer. I chuckle. "Well, we haven't set a date yet. We were waiting until I felt comfortable with…"

Beth grabs my hand and assures me, "We'll be there for you whenever you decide."

"I think I'm ready. He's been so patient with me."

A few hours later, I'm finally handing the credit card over, and I have a genuine smile plastered on my face. Sara comes up behind me and wraps her arms around my waist and pulls me close her.

"You look so beautiful in that dress. Caston is going to flip when he sees you."

Having her arms around me, I flush slightly. "I'm already nervous, and we haven't even set a date yet."

"You have nothing to worry about."

Pulling myself together, I text Caston that I found a dress. I know he'll be happy to hear it. Grabbing the bag of sexy lingerie I bought to surprise Cass with, I check my phone to see if I have a response yet. He hasn't even read the message. I start to get a funny feeling in the pit of my stomach. Something isn't right.

Sara and Beth are waiting for me. Walking through the doors, I suddenly feel light headed. A chill runs through my body, and I break out in a cold sweat. My chest feels constricted, and my stomach flips. I cover my mouth, turn to the bushes, and proceed to lose the contents of my stomach.

Feeling hands on my back, I know Sara is there. I sink to the ground, wiping my mouth with the back of my hand.

"What's wrong, honey?"

I shake my head. "I don't know what came over me. Maybe the champagne isn't agreeing with me."

"Let's get you home."

Looking at my phone again, I still don't have a text back from Caston. It makes my already churning stomach clench again.

Sara helps me up and walks me back to the car. Beth hands me a bottle of water and wipes my forehead with a cool cloth that she got from the ladies in the bridal store. "You guys are too nice to me."

Beth hugs me. "Bre, we love you."

"That was so weird. It came on all of a sudden."

Sara gets into the driver seat and starts the car. "I just sent a text to Caston to tell him we're on our way back."

"Has he responded?" I ask Sara.

"No, why?"

"I sent a text to him before I left the store, and he still has yet to respond. That isn't like him."

"Definitely not," Sara says as she eases her way onto the highway.

Beth rubs my shoulders from the backseat. "I'm sure he's just busy, Sabrina."

I hear the worry in her voice, and Sara's biting her lip as if she's worried too. I try not to think negatively and lean my head back. Taking deep breaths, I will my stomach to settle. The sky is beginning to darken with storm clouds and it racks my nerves more than I want to admit. Something is off, I'm just not sure what.

Chapter Eleven

Caston

James and I stare at each other, neither one flinching. My jaw is tense. Finally, he looks away.

"Caston, I helped Rose disappear. I've also been in contact with her all these years."

"WHAT?" I threw my glass behind him, smashing it to a thousand pieces making him jump. His head flies around to catch my gaze.

Eyes wide he says, "Now, please, don't. Let's just calm down."

Seriously, he is trying to calm me after he tells me he has been keeping my mother from me for twenty-two years. Lunging toward him I drag my own father up by the neck of his shirt and bring him within inches of my face.

"Don't you fucking dare tell me to calm down. You are nothing to me anymore, James. NOTHING!" I finish through gritted teeth.

I see him flinch when I say that. It's true. He has lied to me all these years, kept me away from my mother, and kept me in the hands of that bitch this whole time. He obviously has no respect for me, no love. I shove him back down onto the couch.

"Listen, when I finally came to my senses Rose was gone again! After she was gone for a few years Beverly filed the paperwork to get Rose legally declared dead. I was devastated thinking I'd never see her again. Then one day out of the blue I got a call from a hospital halfway across the country. They explained that there was a Jane Doe that was badly hurt and was repeating my name and number. I didn't understand what was happening. Immediately getting a feeling that it was Rose, I left for what everyone thought was a business trip. I was taken aback when I walked in that room and it was her. She was beaten, cut, broken—mentally and physically. I feared for Rose's safety now that I'd found her again, I couldn't just leave her. She was the one. You must understand now that you have found Sabrina."

I stand staring at him dumbfounded.

Pacing the room I can't even listen to him. "Do you actually think I believe all this? You are so full of shit."

Not missing a beat he continued, "Once Rose was well enough to make sense, she told me Beverly and some men came to her apartment a few days after I took you. She said Beverly told the men to 'take care of her'. They covered her head and beat her, then they sold her to someone. Her 'master' held her hostage in a concrete cell off of a basement. How she actually got to the hospital we still don't know to this day. No one in the ER knew other than she'd been brought in by a Good Samaritan, and Rose didn't remember anything. I got her set up in a private hospital when she was well enough physically to be transferred. They worked with her try to make her who she was years ago. She was scared of everything. She was just a shell of a woman. It was horrible watching her mentally breaking down."

Running my hands through my hair, I contemplate how this crazy story has to be true. He hasn't stopped, and my questions haven't thrown him. I lean on the bar again and cross my arms over my chest to continue listening.

"Working with a private lawyer, so Beverly wouldn't know, I got Rose set up with a new name and life. It took many years at that hospital for her to get back to somewhat normal. I would take regular trips to see her. We spent many years talking about you and what you've been up too. I took her pictures and videos of important events."

Seething through gritted teeth, "You knew for years that that Beverly was fucking with me. You left me with her. In her claws to do with as she pleased while you ran off."

"Caston, I wasn't aware of all the fucked up things Beverly was doing to you. I lived with rose colored glasses on. I wanted to believe she loved you, like she loved Jon. That the sacrifices Rose and I made weren't in vain. I can't tell you how sorry I am. Please, believe me."

We are silent for quite some time. The tension in the room was so thick you could cut it with a knife. How could I ever forgive him? I thought I already had, but he was still lying to me then. Now that I know the real story…

"Were you ever going to tell me?" I whisper under my breath as I scrub my hands over my face.

"Marie and I… I mean Rose and I have talked it over many times, but we could never find a way to do it to ensure her safety from Beverly. Understand that since Beverly had Rose declared deceased through unlawful means if anyone found out Rose was alive, there would be legal consequences for everyone involved for defrauding the government. Not to mention, Beverly would most definitely make sure Rose was 'taken care of' this time. And Rose knew Beverly would include you, as well, this time. Her fear for your safety was the biggest factor. She wouldn't risk you. When Beverly had Rose taken the last thing she told Rose was 'I'll have your son. He will love me as his mother, and James will love me for that. They will both forget you.' We both thought that Beverly was satisfied by taking you away from Rose.

"Anytime I broached the subject Mar—Rose would have a panic attack. Sometimes the attacks were so severe she would end up back in the hospital. She's virtually a recluse; rarely going any further than her back yard. She has a live-in-companion to help take care of her. Rose is still merely a shell of the vibrant woman you remember, Cass, but she's come so far from where she was. It's killed both of us keeping this secret from you. I hoped the older you became she would be able to see you were safe, and she could be a part of your life. But her fear is deeply engrained. She hasn't ever confided in me what happened to her, but she did allow her doctors to tell me some of her recollections. Cass, no one should ever have to be subjected to the things she was. Those memories were always in her mind. She could never consider something like that being done to you. There are worse fates than death.

"I don't know how she's going to handle all of this. I'm actually not sure how anyone found out that she was still alive. We thought we had everything covered up. But, please, Cass, try to understand where she is coming from. Wouldn't you do anything to protect Sabrina?" He must see the fear flash in my eyes, because he continues, "Now imagine if that was your child."

I feel the bile rising in my throat. I swallow hard to keep from losing it. How could they have thought I would be safe in Beverly's clutches?

My heart is racing, and my breathing becomes shallow. I'm on the verge of a panic attack. I have to get out of here.

"Don't fucking leave. Don't you even think about it." I storm out of the room and walk out onto the patio. I lean forward, rest my hands on knees, and take a deep cleansing breath. Terrance appears quickly behind me.

"Terrance, don't let him leave, even if it means you have to restrain him."

"Yes, sir."

I walk further down the yard to the lake. Staring out over the water I watch the thunder heads roll in. I hear the rumbling in the distance and see the lightning snake through the clouds. My mood reflects the incumbent weather. As if Sabrina knew I needed her, my phone chimes that a text from her has come through.

My heart aches with love for her. I can't wait to make her my wife and start a new life together. An uncomplicated, perfect life. I laugh at the thought. Uncomplicated, what the fuck is that?

I've never run from my problems. My life has been one fucked up event after another. How am I supposed to bring Sabrina into my life and make everything perfect for her?

I bend down and pick up a stone, turning it over and over in my hand. Letting out a loud yell, I fling the smooth stone, sending it skipping along the relatively calm water. I fall to my knees as lightning strikes and large rain drops start to fall. I run both hands through my hair, grabbing it roughly.

I feel lost. Unsure. I'm not sure how long I've been kneeling by the lake, it's dark and still raining. I'm soaked to the bone, and my legs fell asleep a long time ago. I take a deep breath, trying to cleanse my thoughts.

I feel her presence before she wraps her arms around me, pulling me into her lap, the warmth of her arms around me, providing the solace I desperately need. I turn my face into her chest, inhaling another deep breath. We sit on the sand, letting the rain continue to soak us to the bone. She tightens her embrace and strokes my back, lightly kissing my temple.

"Cass," she whispers lightly, "baby, I'm here for you. I'm not going anywhere."

She tightens her embrace, and I look up into her hazel eyes. She leans forward and kisses me gently.

"I love you, Sabrina."

"I love you too, Caston." Her eyes twinkle and she smiles. She looks a little pale.

I capture her mouth in mine, sweeping my tongue along her bottom lip, nibbling lightly. We start to deepen the kiss as another large lightning bolt strikes. Sabrina jumps back out of our embrace, clutching her chest. I chuckle as she gives me a look that makes me smirk.

"This storm is getting bad, Cass. Let's go back to the house."

"Little bit longer, okay? I just can't go back in there yet."

She nods as she let me wrap her in my arms this time. Sabrina strokes the hair on the back of my neck, allowing me time to regain my composure.

I feel her breathing increase as I lightly nibble on her neck. A shiver runs through her, and I pull her head back to look up at me. "Bre, I need you."

Her pale skin flushes as she looks around. "Here, now?"

I nod. "No one can see us."

"But, your dad—"

I cut her off as I press my mouth to hers. My tongue searches, seeking hers. Shifting her slightly, I reach for the hem of her top and pull it over her head. Unhooking her bra, I pull it down and secure her hands behind her. Her breath catches and a small groan comes from her. My dick is throbbing, begging to be released. The rain falling over her breasts makes them look even more delicious than they already were. I lean forward, licking the drops. Her nipples call to me. I take one of the buds in my mouth and tug. Grabbing it between my teeth, I pull, grazing it as I pop the nipple free.

"God, Caston. Please."

"What do you need, baby?"

She looks at me, her eyes twinkling. "You."

Lust clouds my vision. I release her hands and remove my shirt. She takes advantage by pushing me down slowly to the beach behind me and rising above me. She's beautiful. Her small hands slowly undo my pants. She starts to pull them down, but stops and kisses me below my belt line. I slide my hands into her hair and pull her up to me.

Our kisses are hungry and hurried. Reaching down, I bunch her skirt up around her waist and reach for her pussy. Moving the thong to the side, I let my fingers sink into her.

"Fuck, Bre, you're so wet."

Her hands slide along my legs, pushing my pants down around my thighs. My cock springs free. I apply a little pressure on her clit, and she whimpers. Her hands grasp my hard shaft, and she leans forward to take me into her mouth. She lets my cock hit the back of her throat. The rumble of her moan makes me thrust harder into her mouth.

I withdraw quickly and pull her up to my mouth again.

"Bre, if I don't fuck you right now, I'm going to lose it."

The rain is still falling over us, but neither of us care.

"Caston, I need you too."

I pull her on top of me, shifting her so we don't irritate her leg. My cock is posed at her entrance. I hesitate just a moment to take in the angel poised above me.

"Cass, what's wrong?"

Before she can second guess me or herself, I plunge into her, making her scream. I take her hard and fast. She's so wet for me. Her velvet folds caress my cock. Holding on to her hips to keep her still, I continue my assault. "Fuck yes." A growl goes through me. I can't hold on much longer. Sabrina places her hands over mine, and I lace our fingers together.

"God, Caston, I'm coming," Sabrina yells as her head falls back, and her pussy milks my cock.

My balls tighten against my body, and I still my thrusting as I spill into her. She falls over my body, and I wrap my arms around her. The rain continues to fall on us. The relaxing sound of the droplets hitting the water in the lake calms me. I lightly stroke her back as we both come down from our high. Still connected I feel her pussy grip me when it spasms again from her orgasm.

"Bre, I could lay with you like this forever."

She turns her head into the crook of my neck and kisses lightly. Her lips travel up my neck to my ear. She nibbles on my earlobe, and my cock begins to harden again.

Chapter Twelve

Mark

Turning off on to a side street, I decide I'll catch up to them later. I know they couldn't see me, but I figured once they started driving erratically something was up. I didn't want to risk her calling in her lover and his posse. I was able to install a tracking device on her soon to be sister-in-law's car a few weeks ago, so I'll keep track of them from my phone, instead of tailing them.

I turn into a parking lot and pull out my phone. Bringing up the app the tracking device is linked to, I login and immediately a red dot comes up on the screen. Smiling because I know exactly where they are. Beth, poor unsuspecting Beth, guess I'll make a pit stop at her house to bug her shit too, even though I have some help on the inside, you can never have too much information.

I roll down my windows and takeout a new pack of cigarettes. Damn, I love warm fall days. Hitting them on my knee, I look around and see a redhead walking down the street. I rub my teeth along my bottom lip as I watch her ass sway back and forth in a short skirt. What I wouldn't love to do to her. My cock starts to strain in my pants, and I decide to do something about it.

Jumping out of the SUV, I shove the keys in my pocket and get a cigarette out of the pack. I jog lightly to catch up to her.

"Miss, excuse me." I apply the charm.

Getting closer still, she tries to ignore me. "Miss, do you have a light?"

She looks over at me, and I flash her my boy-next-door smile while tightening my pec muscles, so they're clearly visible under my dark t-shirt. I see her flush slightly and know I've got her now.

"Are you talking to me?" she says while gesturing to herself, pointing directly at her over abundant cleavage. She has an accent, Irish maybe?

I nod. "Yes, sweetheart, do you have a light?"

She giggles and blushes. "No, I don't smoke."

My cock desperately wants to be free even more now. Irish accent, body to die for—fuck me. "I should quit anyways." I laugh as I put the cigarette behind my ear. "What brings you to town?"

"Work." She blushes slightly. "I'm only in town for a week. Computer stuff."

"Hot damn, no shit." *Fuck me, I need you now.*

She smiles and fidgets.

Holding out my hand to her, I start our introductions, "My name is Mark, and you are?"

That pink blush comes over her again. "Kaitlyn." She holds her hand out to me. I grab it, pulling it up to my lips, lightly kissing the back of her hand. She takes a deep breath to try to calm herself. I'm affecting her. I bet, if we were indoors, I could smell her arousal.

"Look, you don't know me, but I'd love to show you around, dinner maybe?" *Fuck you hard against the door of your hotel room and never talk to you again.*

Her smile gets wider. "I was just on my way for a late light lunch before heading back to the office. I was going to—oh where is that paper?" She digs through her bag for a small piece of paper with the name of a local deli on it. Locating it, she holds it out for me to read.

"Ah, yes. They have some great sandwiches." I offer my arm to her, and she links hers with mine. I've got her now.

We make chit chat as we walk down the street just a few blocks to the deli. I pull out my phone and check the location of Bre and Sara. Still at Beth's–good. Turning back to my date of the minute, I open the door for her, and we walk up to the counter. Never missing a beat, we order our food and continue on to pay. I start feeling around for my wallet like an idiot.

"My God, I forgot my wallet at home. How stupid."

She giggles and pats my shoulder. "No worries, I've got it."

I grab the tray and walk to the outside seating. Being past lunch but not quite dinner it's pretty empty.

"I'm so sorry. Can you forgive me?" I push out my lower lip into a full puppy dog pout.

"Of course, but you must do me one thing."

Pulling the paper back on the sandwich I respond, "Sure, baby, what's that?" *Baby because I already forgot your name.*

"Take me out tonight?"

I nearly choked on my sandwich. "What?" I said, clearing my throat.

She moves the salad around in the bowl. I like that she eats light. I like a woman that makes me feel strong. Since I didn't answer her question, she's looking downward and won't make eye contact. Very good, baby girl.

"Baby, look at me."

She glances up and her eyes are moist. God damn, she's perfect.

I reach over and caress her chin. "Baby, I can't tonight, but how about tomorrow?"

Shifting in her seat, she smiles. "Okay, Mark." I cup her cheek, taking in the velvety feeling of her skin, a few seconds before going back to eat my sandwich.

I check the phone again and see they're on the move. Fuck. Pushing my sandwich away, I look up to her. "Baby, where's your hotel?"

Her breath catches, and I see her start breathing heavy. "Few blocks back," she whispers.

I nod my head in that direction. "Let's get out of here."

She giggles as she stands up, and I stand guiding her toward the hotel. I smack her ass and give it a good squeeze as she hops, turning to walk backward. Snaking my arm around her waist, I pull her to me. She slides her hands around my neck and plays with the blond curls at the nape of my neck. A low growl comes from my throat. "Fuck, baby, my cock is so damn hard."

I reach around and grab both of her ass cheeks in my hands. At least I'll have a fuck buddy for a few days, and she's hot, even better. Getting some sideways glances from us walking down the sidewalk, groping each other, I turn her down the next alleyway. I can't wait any longer.

Taking her mouth, I devour her lips. They're soft and smooth. The moan that she lets out vibrates into my mouth. Fuck this sensitive shit. I pick her up, and she wraps her legs around my waist. Walking her behind the dumpster, I back her up to the wall. She grinds herself on my cock that's begging to be let out. Since her back is supported, I'm able to push her skirt up and let my fingers find her hot cunt. Fuck me, she's so damn wet. I'm momentarily sidetracked by her mouth skimming its way along my jaw up to my ear.

Unzipping, I pop my cock out and slam into her. She's so fucking slick and warm. Her velvety insides grip me. Her yell does things to me. I keep the pace up hard and quick. Feeling my balls start to squeeze to my body, I slip out of her, dropping her legs and shoving her down to her knees. She gasps at my abrupt withdrawal. I ball my hand in the red curls at the back of her head and shove her mouth over my cock. She sucks generously. It only takes a few pumps before I'm spilling my come down her throat.

"Fuck, baby, swallow it. Don't let anything spill."

When I'm empty, I pull her up by her hair. I know she didn't come, but that wasn't my point. I needed to get off, I don't give a fuck about her.

"Thanks for that, baby. I'll come back for you tomorrow. Same time, same deli. Got it."

I shove myself back in my pants and kiss her cheek before she can answer. Licking my fingers that I'd shoved into her earlier, I take in her taste. "You taste so fucking good, baby."

Her surprised face turns into a devilish smile from the compliment.

I turn to leave, but before I do I stop. I wonder how far she is willing to go for me. "Baby, instead of meeting me here, I'll meet you at the hotel. What's your room number?"

I see her swallow hard, not sure if she should tell me. I walk back over to her, slide my hand in her hair and pull her to me, devouring her mouth. Leaving her breathless when I back away, she whispers, "Five thirty-four."

"Good girl." With that I turn and jog back out to the street and take off toward the SUV.

Getting in, I grab one of the cigarettes and light it up, taking a deep inhale. My phone chimes, and I remove it from my pocket.

Seeing they are moving, I quickly turn out of the lot and head in that direction.

In no time their car appears in my line of sight. They have Beth with them now. I pull my sunglasses off the visor and slide them on. I keep my distance this time, so they don't see me.

Once they are at the bridal store, I cringe. I don't want anything to do with this. Confirming that they actually go into the store, I wait about five minutes before heading back to Beth's apartment.

The drive over to her apartment is like second nature. All of the times I traveled between the frat house and her place with Broc, I could make this trip using only muscle memory. My supposed best friend, who fucking disappeared after shit went down with Sabrina going to Caston.

Pulling up to the front of Beth's apartment, I park the car and take in my surroundings. The sky rumbles. Looking up, I can see a storm brewing in the distance. Sliding out of the car, I quickly make my way up to the door. Stopping before I get there, I glance behind me, making sure no one was looking. I pull out the gloves in my pocket. Sliding my hand along the top of the door jamb, my hand hits the cold metal key sitting in the same fucking place it's been for the last three years.

A devious smile crosses my face as the key slides in to the lock and I hear it click as I turn it. Typical, not one damn thing in here has changed.

Moving around her furniture, I find her computer sitting on the coffee table. Grabbing it I quickly open it to see it immediately bring up her home screen. I laugh that people don't even consider having a password on their personal shit, not that it would have stopped me. Installing a tracking device, I return it to its place on the table before going through some of her other belongings.

Finishing up, I head to the front door. Letting myself out, I quickly make my way to the SUV and slide into the driver's seat. The phone shows that the girls are still at the bridal salon, so I decide to head home. The weather looks like it's going to get bad, so I'll just continue to monitor them from my phone.

Letting myself into my condo, I unload my pockets onto the table by the door. I take a deep breath and roll my head on my shoulders. The place is quiet. Beverly must not be here.

I strip off my shirt and jeans as I walk through the condo to the bedroom. Falling on to the bed face first, I'm so exhausted sleep takes over me.

The knock at my door wakes me from my sleep. Running my hands through my hair before I rub the stubble on my chin as I walk through the beer cans and clothes thrown on the floor of my room. Yawning, I pull the door open.

"What the fuck…" I stop mid-sentence. Standing before me is one of the most beautiful women I've ever seen. She's obviously older, but damn is she HOT! "How you doin'?" I smirk.

"Mark, I presume?"

I prop myself on the doorframe. Her sexy body is making my cock stand at attention and being only in my boxers I have one hell of a tent going on. I cross my arms over my chest. "Who wants to know?"

Her jaw tenses, and she pushes by me. The smell of jasmine fills my nostrils and a groan leaves me. She turns around and rolls her eyes at me. "Mark, close the door."

"You still haven't told me who you are, beautiful."

She steps close to me. Her head leans toward mine, and I feel the warmth of her breath on my neck. "You have something I want, and I am something you need."

She nibbles at my ear and suddenly her hand smacks down onto my cock, sending a jolt of pain through me making me want to fall to my knees. A squeeze on my hard shaft sends another wave of pain through me, this time making me harder than I thought possible. I slide my hand into her hair and pull her back into me, taking her mouth in mine. Her tongue fights for dominancy. Finally she delivers a hot stinging slap crosses my face.

"You will call me Mistress."

Still maintaining her hold on my cock, she leads me to my bed. She shoves me down on the mattress and stands before me, taking in her surroundings before moving to the desk. She sits gracefully in the chair, crossing her legs slowly. I groan again when I notice the lace of her stockings peeking out from the skirt that has ridden up.

"My name is Beverly Holden, but you will never call me by my real name. I need your help with something that is very near and dear to me." Her voice is like velvet. "If you help me, I'll allow you to have me."

Letting out a laugh, I let my head fall back. "Look, lady, I'm not sure who you are, but I have plenty of women wanting to climb on this."

Her face shows her disgust, and she once again rolls her eyes. "Bull shit!"

I get up and walk over to her, standing over her. Normally women cower when I do this, she didn't even flinch.

"Sit the fuck down, NOW!"

I back up and take a seat, glancing down at my feet.

"Good boy, you may look at me again."

Looking up, her face is still hardened.

"Beverly Holden? I don't know that name."

She chuckles. "I bet you know Caston Black."

Is she serious right now? What sick joke is this? "That fucker stole my life.

He took everything from me, but what's it to you?"

A Grinch-like smile crosses her face. "More than you know. I think we can work well together. That is, if you're willing to get your hands dirty for me."

Beverly continues to talk about the relationship she had with Caston and how he spited her. She's looking for revenge and explains how I come into her plan.

I scratch my chin and stand up to stretch. I pace the room, thinking about what she's saying to me. Could I really do this?

The next pass I make by her, she grabs my cock. Completely catching me by surprise, I clinch the back of her head and shove her head onto my shaft. Her warm mouth slides up and down, making me want to fall to my knees. Before I'm able to come, she pushes me back.

"What the fuck, lady?"

"You like that? There's more where that came from. I can definitely teach things you've never dreamed of. Why don't you just say yes, pretty boy, so we can just move on with my plans?"

Nodding my head slowly, she gets up from the chair and makes her way to me, unbuttoning her top as she approaches. Using her shirt she ties my hands together before I can make a move on her.

"What the—"

"No talking."

"But—"

SMACK. "I said no talking! You will from this point on only call me Mistress and only talk when you are being addressed. Do you understand?"

Eyes wide, I stare back at her. "What?"

She steps back and smacks me again. "I will not proceed until you address me the correct way."

I have to have her. I've never been this hard in my life. "Yes—yes, Mistress."

Her evil smile appears again. "Good boy. Let's see how I can take care of this for you."

She leans over me and sinks her mouth onto my cock again. I groan and let *my eyes close, relishing in her expert mouth and thinking about the deal I just made with the devil.*

The jingling of the phone breaks through my dream. I turn my head toward the noise and reach around, feeling next to me until I find the vibrating, annoying sound. Cracking one of my eyes open, I see that Sara's car is on the move again. Groaning, I squeeze my eyes shut again and roll over, so I can stretch before getting up. My cock is standing on high alert because of the dream I just woke from. I grab my shaft in my hand and rub it up and down. Fuck, I wish Beverly was here or the redhead. Her lips were like heaven.

Rolling off of the bed, I shuffle my way to the bathroom to take a shower. Beverly's payments for doing her dirty work let me get a condo nicer than any place I've ever lived in before. The room starts to fill with steam, and I step under the stream of water. Turning my face into the hot liquid, I slowly rest my head onto the tile wall. The wheels in my head start turning on how I'm going to execute the next part of my plan.

A laugh rises up through my body at my choice of words, execute. Laughing aloud and having the sound echo through the room makes it evil sounding. I guess I am for what I have planned.

Chapter Thirteen

Caston

After making love to Sabrina on our beach, I lay with her resting on my chest, listening to the rain splash on the water. The sound is calming and Bre was curled into me on the verge of falling asleep. I look up into the sky and watch the rain fall down on us.

Even through the calm my mind is racing. What am I going to do about James… about Rose? How am I going to handle the situation that lies ahead of me—us now?

Sabrina shivers and curls tighter into the crook of my arm. Mindlessly, I stroke her arm and her skin relaxes under my touch. I hear an owl in the distance, and the lighting streaks across the sky again.

Shifting slightly, I grab my soaked t-shirt and pull it over Sabrina's head before moving to stand. I pull my jeans up then crouch down to her. Pushing her soaked hair off her forehead, her eyes meet mine. I smile and think how perfect life is with her. She takes in a deep breath when I lean over to place a kiss where my fingers just passed. I scoop her up into my arms, and she laces her hands around my neck.

I slowly make my way back to the house. Terrance meets me halfway with a blanket to wrap around Sabrina.

"Thank you, Terrance."

He nods. "I have James in the den waiting for you. Bruce, the new hire that will be helping with security around the office, is waiting with him."

We turn to continue walking to the house in silence. Reaching the French doors, Terrance opens them for me. I step into the house and head for the stairs.

"I'll be back down in a few minutes. Let me get her settled. Please, let James know."

"Yes, sir."

Terrance takes off in the opposite direction, and I start the climb to our room.

Once in our room, I lay her on the bed. I place a chaste kiss on her lips before I step away to grab a towel to dry her hair.

Returning to her, I see Sabrina has discarded my shirt and her ivory skin has a beautiful gleam to it. Sitting beside her, I slowly start to towel dry her hair by separating sections and blotting them lightly.

I lift her into my chest and start rubbing her shoulders before sliding my hands down the front of her body to knead her breasts. Her head falls back on my shoulder, but her eyes stay shut. I lean forward and kiss her. Her lips part, letting our tongues dance over each other. I pull away, guiding her down to the pillow again and bring the covers up over her sexy body before tucking her in.

"Stay." The word is breathless, barely a whisper.

Tucking her locks behind her ear, I lean down to kiss her cheek. "I'll be back before you know it."

"Mmm hum…" she mumbles incoherently, "Caston?"

"Yes, baby. What do you need?" I whisper.

"I want to set a date."

Smiling, I kiss her forehead. "In the morning. Sleep now."

I've been asking her to set a date for a while now, but she was reluctant because of how she walks. Today must have been good for her to feel comfortable enough to set a date. I'm elated that she's finally ready, but it's late, and she can barely stay awake. She shifts and slides further down into the sheets.

Pushing my hands through my hair, I walk into my closet to grab dry clothes before heading back down to James. Collecting my thoughts, I finally head toward the den.

Terrance and Bruce stand by the door until I walk in.

"I'll only be a minute, then you can show Mr. Holden out of my house."

Terrance steps away, nodding his understanding.

James sits up straighter when I walk toward him. I have so many thoughts going through my head. I'm not even sure where to start, or if I even want too.

"Son." He holds his arms out to me, trying to apologize.

"Don't." Stopping him. "Listen to me, and listen good; I want you to leave. I need time to think about what you've told me. What happens from here I can't say." I stop, not knowing what I really want to say.

"I'm so sorry, Caston. It was for hers and your safety. Please, try to understand that your mother isn't mentally stable."

My head snaps up. "That excuses her, but what about you? You're sane. Was it worth sacrificing your son to have your lover?" I stop, taking a deep breath to try to calm my nerves.

"Caston, it wasn't like that. I saw what Beverly wanted me to see. I never thought she could do the things she did to you. Why do you think she always waited until I was gone? Once you came to live with us and Rose was gone, it was like Beverly's need for vengeance ceased. I thought she was better. I thought she loved you, like she loved Jon." On the verge of sobbing, he takes several deep breaths before whispering. "I just never knew how far she would go."

"I can't get into this anymore right now. I don't know what to think of what you've told me." Turning, I walk out of the room, knowing Terrance will make sure James makes it home.

Chapter Fourteen

Sabrina

I wake up to the sun shining on my face. The warm body snuggled up to my back is comforting, and the breeze coming in the open windows makes me take a deep cleansing breath, letting the fresh air fill my lungs. I try to move, but Caston groans and pulls me into him tighter.

"I don't even remember coming to bed last night." I sleepily whisper, turning my head into the pillow as my stomach does flip flops when Caston's hand starts traveling down grazing the top of my sex.

Hot kisses start along the back of my shoulders and between kisses he says, "You were—so sated—you fell asleep—when your head hit the pillow." He reaches my earlobe and nibbles gently, making me laugh lightly. "I carried you up to bed and tucked you in." Whispering in my ear, his hot breath is sending pulses of desire to my pussy.

"Thank you, darling." I turn my face toward him and try to speak in some sort of accent.

He leans back and starts laughing. "God, I love you so much."

I sit up and look over at him, shaking my head. "What happened with your dad?"

He suddenly stops laughing and swings his legs over the side of the bed. The muscles in his back ripple as he scrubs his hands over his face. "God, Bre. It's such a cluster fuck. I don't even know what I'm going to do."

I get up on my knees and scoot behind him. I start rubbing his shoulders while I kiss them lightly. "You can tell me anything, you know?"

Caston's muscles are so tight. I feel bad that this is making him uneasy. His moans indicate my little massage feels good.

"I know I can tell you. I'm just not sure how to even explain it." He sounds so melancholy.

I reach around and clasp my arms around his neck as I lean over and kiss his cheek. Caston grabs my arms and quickly stands up with me attached on his back. Letting out a screech, I quickly wrap my legs around his waist. "Caston! Put me down. What are you doing? Caston!"

Without a word he carries me into the bathroom over to our large soaking tub and bends over to start the water. I use my feet to tease his cock, trying to get him to set me down.

"Bre, that isn't going to work."

"Baby, please, put me down."

Caston continues to walk around the bathroom, collecting things for the bath. When the tub is almost full he adds a little bubble bath that instantly starts to foam and sends the aromatic scents of lavender and vanilla through the air.

Finally seeming satisfied, he walks over to the double sinks, setting me down, so I'm sitting on the counter. He turns around in my arms and takes my mouth in a kiss that sends shivers throughout my whole body. I reach up, sliding my hands through his hair. Enjoying the moans we're humming into each other's mouths. He pulls away breathless. The lustful look in his eyes renders me speechless.

Caston falls to his knees and starts kissing along the insides of my thighs, giving each one equal attention. Slowly getting closer and closer to the place I want his mouth more than anything.

As he reaches my pussy, he flicks my clit with the tip of his tongue, sending bolts of lightning down my legs. I let my head fall back as I give myself over to his expert tongue. Sucking, flicking, and driving me insane. I was about to come when he pulls back. "No, my God, please don't stop."

Not acknowledging my plea, he stands up and pulls me to him. Reaching around, he holds me by my ass and carries me to the tub. Stepping into the bubbles, we slink down into the warmth. Leaning back Caston turns the water off and immediately turns his attention back to me by taking my breasts in his hands, kneading them and pinching my nipples between his fingers.

"Bre, do you know how beautiful you are?" His eyes are a dark and hooded with lust.

I bite my lip as I let my hands slide through his hair. Breathless, I pant, "Caston…"

He shifts slightly and pulls me up over his lap, setting me down on his hard cock. The water sloshes around us, spilling onto the floor with our movement. Reaching around his neck, I let my fingers slide through Caston's steam dampened hair as his mouth trails kisses along my neck. As his tongue glides along my jaw up to my ear, I'm pushed over the edge.

His cock pulses, filling me. My womb flutters, and my heart wants to explode. I lean forward to rest in his arms.

We sit in silence for a long time. Occasionally, Caston turns the water on to bring the temperature back up. Once I turn around and lean my back on Caston's chest, I can feel his heart. I toe at one of the jets at the end of the tub as Caston lightly strokes my arms.

Just as I feel myself start to drift off to sleep again, Caston starts talking.

"James has been hiding my mom for years. She's still alive, but is terrified to see me. He says she was kidnapped and held as a slave by Beverly's command. My mom managed to get free and seek help. James says that her fear is deep, and that she's scared Beverly might punish me if her existence came to light."

After filling me in on everything that went down between him and James last night, my heart breaks for him. The only time in his life when things weren't complicated was when he was with Rose the first four years of his life. Tears start falling down my cheeks.

His arms tighten around me as he finishes. We sit in silence a little while longer. I'm not sure exactly what to say.

Caston shifts and kisses me on the top of my head. "Sorry to bring you down."

I lean over to the side and turn my head toward him. "Cass, don't be sorry."

He closes his eyes and lets his head fall back onto the bath pillow behind him. "My whole life has been a lie. Fake and so fucked up."

I turn around quickly, sending water over the edge of the tub again. Taking his head in my hands, I pull his face to look at me. "Stop it."

His eyes fly open to look at me.

"I'll be with you the whole way."

He sits up and wraps his arms around my waist. "What did I do to deserve you?"

A small smile graces my lips. "I could ask you the same question."

I worry my lip when I remember what I told him last night.

"What's wrong, Bre?"

"I want to get married after Beverly's trial. So, in about two months."

I can tell he's shocked. "So soon? Don't get me wrong, I'll marry you right now, but don't you have to have time to plan all this stuff?"

"I hope you aren't mad, but I talked with Sara and Beth about it yesterday, and they agreed to help me with all the details. Plus, if we get a wedding coordinator—"

Stopping me with a kiss, he leans back. "Bre, this is your day. If you want to get married in two months, then two months it will be."

I hear his phone ringing in the distance. Feeling him tense up in my arms, I know he hears it too. Taking a deep breath, he moves to get out of the tub. His long limbs stretch to get the fluffy white towel. He wraps it around his waist before he walks out into the main room to collect his ringing phone.

Looking at how wrinkled my fingers are, I decide to get out of the water as well. Sliding my legs over the side, I dry off with a towel before wrapping it around my head and donning my robe.

I walk over to the sinks and reach forward, wiping the steam of the mirror. Just as my face comes into view my vision is filled with flashing lights, and I lean forward catching myself on the countertop.

"Bre, are you okay?"

Caston is by my side in a matter of seconds. He quickly scoops me up and carries me to the bed.

I close my eyes and continue taking deep breaths.

"Bre, talk to me, you're scaring me."

I reach over and grab his hand. Taking one last deep breath, a shiver goes through me. "I'm okay now. I don't know what came over me. Probably the hot water and all the steam combined with me getting out of the tub so fast. I'm sorry I scared you."

Pulling my hand up to his lips, he kisses it lightly. "Don't fucking do that to me."

I chuckle. "I'll do my best."

He sits by my side for a little while longer before he speaks tentatively. "I don't think you should go into work today after what just happened."

I see him cringe, thinking I'm going to fight him on this, but still feeling a little shaky I think he may be right.

"I think you're right. I'm still not feeling the best. I'm sorry, Caston."

He sighs, his relief obvious. "Nothing to be sorry for, Sabrina."

He leans over to kiss me on the head before he heads to the closet to finish getting ready for work. I slide under the covers, "Maybe I'll call Sara and have her take me to the doctor."

"I can take you." Looking concerned as he dresses for work.

"No, no. I'm sure it's nothing. I'm going to get a few more hours of sleep before I call them."

Later in the afternoon, I'm sitting in the cold sterile room of my doctor's office. They wanted me to come in right away when I told them what I'd experienced the last few days. Their concern didn't do anything to calm my nerves.

Sara sat on the cold plastic chair in the corner, flipping through a magazine. "Why didn't you tell me you weren't feeling well?" She looks up at me, her face filled with concern.

"I didn't even tell Caston."

We're interrupted by the nurse coming in to take my vitals. As she's handing me a cup, I raise an eyebrow at her. "What's this for?"

"I need a urine sample," she says point blank.

"What exactly do you need with that?" I slide off the table before heading to the bathroom.

"Because we need to rule out that you aren't pregnant."

Sara's head pops up, and my head swings around so hard I might have whiplash. "That's not possible," I murmur.

The nurse chuckles. "Anything's possible."

I'm really ticked off now because she obviously didn't read my file. I slam the little cup down on the table, making Sara and the nurse jump.

"No, it's not. It's not because if you'd read my file and do your fucking job, you'd know that I can't get pregnant."

I hear Sara's breath catch.

She closes the laptop and glares back at me. "Actually, I did read your file. Anything is possible, Ms. Bennett."

I just stare at her mouth open. Grabbing the small cup, I take off down the hall to the restroom.

Stepping out of the room, she holds her latex covered hand out for me to hand her the sample. "I've laid a gown on the table, please remove your clothes and put gown on, opening in the front. Dr. Dana will be in soon."

Making my way back to the room, I'm speechless as I change into the gown. Sara's watching every move I make. I climb up onto the table and cross my ankles. I purposely avoid Sara's gaze.

"Bre?"

Here it comes.

"Why didn't you tell me?"

I look over to her. "Not something that just comes up in normal conversation." I chuckle mirthlessly.

"Does Caston know?" She sounds so concerned.

Sighing. "Yes, he knows. He's known for a while."

I see her release a breath. "What happened?"

Giving her the quick version, she's in tears in a matter of seconds. Rushing to me, hugging the air out of my lungs. "Sara, I'm fine."

She nods and steps back when the doctor walks in.

"You're not pregnant." I laugh because that was the first thing that came out of her mouth.

"Could have told you that."

She shakes her head. "Sabrina, anything is possible. You have damaged fallopian tubes which would make it extremely difficult for you to get pregnant, not that you can't get pregnant. Please, don't use that as a form of birth control."

Shaking my head. "I'm on the pill."

She nods and marks in my file. The appointment goes on without a hitch. Sara and I walk to the car a half an hour later. I pull my phone out and dial Caston.

"Hey, baby."

"Hey, Cass. She determined it was a bad combination of my medicine causing the dizziness and stuff.

Hearing his sigh of relief, I smile. I know he was worried. "Thank goodness. Is Sara taking you to get new ones?"

"Yes, we're on our way to the pharmacy now."

His voice sounds tense and makes me worry. "Caston, what's wrong?" I hear him sigh into the phone.

"I got the file from James on Rose."

"File?" I question, not understanding.

"The documents from her doctors. God, Sabrina, I don't think I'll ever be able to unsee this. Her years with that—I'm not sure how she's even alive right now."

My hand clutches at my neck. "That bad?"

"So much worse than you're probably even thinking. I don't

understand how someone could be this ruthless. Just reading it makes me question if there is a God."

"Caston, that's awful."

I've been frozen in my spot since leaving the doctor's office. I couldn't bring my feet to move. Caston sounds so upset, I wish I was there to wrap my arms around him and tell him it'll be okay.

"Bre, I think I need to meet her." It's barely a whisper, but I hear it.

Chapter Fifteen

Mark

The next day I walk to the hotel of the redhead and go up to her room. True to her word, she's there. As soon as I knock, she lets me in with a blush coloring her face. Too bad I won't let myself get close to anyone because she would probably be a good one.

"So, what would you like to do?" she asks tentatively.

"When do you have to be back at work?" I ask as I walk to the window, looking out over the city below.

She fidgets with the bottom of her shirt. "Not until seven. We have to wait until everyone is done for the day, so we don't interfere with their working hours."

Since it's only one, we have some time. She slowly walks over to me, unbuttoning her shirt on the way. When she reaches me, she lets it fall open. Grabbing the bottom of my shirt, she pulls it over my head. My mouth crashes into hers, and we're suddenly lost in each other. I slide my hands into her hair, pulling her head back, trailing my kisses down her neck. I kiss along her collarbone and make my way back up the other side back to her neck. I suck her

109

bottom lip in-between my teeth, nibbling it.

Walking her backwards until her legs hit the side of the bed. Last time I was rough and took what I wanted, but since she was true to her word I'll let her come.

I slide the shirt down her arms and move to her shorts. Our mouths haven't parted. Once I get the button undone, I push them down. She isn't wearing any panties, and I could come on the spot.

"Fuck, baby, you are so damn hot."

I lay her out on the bed. She looks up at me, and I kneel between her legs. First lick and I'm a goner. Damn, I'm in trouble. She's sweet as honey. Fuck, I'm falling. How am I going to explain this to Beverly?

I continue my torment on her pussy until she's a writhing mess beneath me.

Standing up, I slide my pants down, and before I know what's happening she stands up, turning the table on me. She turns me around, forcefully pushing me down on the bed. My eyes go wide in shock. Her eyes are wild, and it turns me on. Holy shit.

She begins to climb up my body and as she's straddling me, she leans over taking my mouth with hers. This time it's different. She's the dominant one. Where did this come from? I try to put my hands on her hips, but she grabs at my wrists.

"No, no touching."

"What?"

Her head shakes slowly and a devilish grin flashes across her face. She forcefully pins my hands by my head. Could I over take her? Of course. Will I? Normally, I'd say yes, but for some reason I'm harder than I've been in a long time.

"I'm in control now." Music to my ears. Her accent rings through heavily when she says it, and my cock jumps. "It's my turn to play."

Before I know what's going on, she handcuffs me to the

headboard. My breathing increases, and she moves to straddle me again. Just letting my tip tease her entrance.

"Fuck, baby, I need you wrapped around me."

The red hair flips, and she slowly lowers herself onto me. Suddenly, she gets off of me and walks to the other side of the room. I groan at the loss of her heat. She riffles through a bag before turning back to me.

I see she has a condom. I want nothing more than to let loose inside of her. I laugh because I was inside of her bareback yesterday, but, right now, I don't care.

When she's next to me she slowly unrolls it over my shaft. Thankful that she's slow, because I'm so wound up I could embarrass the hell out of myself.

She looks back at me, her green eyes glowing. "Baby, if you don't get back on me, I'm going to rip this headboard off the wall and come after you."

She giggles, but immediately straightens herself out. I laugh to myself, she's trying so hard to be dominant.

Her legs are on either side of me again, and she slides down slower than she did before. Her head falls back as a moan goes through her body. Once I'm inside her completely, she stills. Wanting her to move, I push up a bit. Her head flips back up, and she glares. Just then her hips start to twist.

"Holy shit." My eyes close, and I grit my teeth.

Once she goes to town riding me, it's all I can do to keep myself from coming too soon. Her breasts bounce hard, and I really want them in my mouth.

"Mark, I'm coming. Oh God!"

I feel her start to pulse around my cock, and my body freezes as my come empties into the condom. She collapses on me, breathing hard. I kiss her forehead, tasting the sweat that has formed on her. My heart aches. This is not good.

"Babe, can you let me go?"

She giggles softly and reaches up to unlatch the cuffs. Once I am undone, she falls back onto my chest. I lift her slightly and remove myself from the warm depths of her body. Reaching down, I pull the condom off and toss it over the side of the bed. Pulling her back to my body, I stroke her back and kiss the top of her head. What the fuck am I getting into?

We lay like that for a little while before we both drift into a short slumber.

Waking up a little while later, I have her cradled against me, her back to my front. Her hair smells like strawberries which makes me laugh because she has red hair. I kiss her shoulder and slowly move away from her to head toward the bathroom.

Once inside, I start the shower and step inside. All I could do was think about her. What the fuck is wrong with me? I lean my head on the tile wall and let the water fall over me. I'm not sure how long I stand there before I hear the door open.

"Mark?"

She slides in behind me and wraps her hands around my waist. I know I need to stop this before she falls too hard. Oh what the fuck am I saying, before I fall too hard.

I instantly turn in her arms and kiss her. She pushes up onto her toes, so she can reach my lips a little better. I do her one better and sweep her off her feet, pressing her to the wall of the shower.

"I need you," I say when I rest my head on her forehead.

She wiggles her hips, and I let myself slide into her slowly. I don't do slow. I've only done slow once in my life. That was with Sabrina at the lake. Pushing that thought out of my head, I continue. My hands kneed her ass, and I feel myself getting close to the edge.

"I'm going to come. Are you close?" I say into her neck between a few kisses and nips.

"Fuck yes, Mark. I need you."

She has no idea what that does to me. I want to come in her so bad, but I won't.

Once I feel her start to convulse around me, I pull out and come on the wall below her. I press my chest to her and take her mouth with mine.

When we come back to earth, I know I need to get the fuck out of here. Now!

Seeing her eyes turn sad when I tell her I have to go hurts. I want nothing more than to crawl back in bed with her and fall asleep again. I need the shit beat out of me. There's only one place to go for that.

I arrive back home and make my way through the condo. Stopping in front of her room, I take a deep breath and open the door. Walking into the room, I see she isn't here, but I need this. I strip down and sit on the floor naked with my head bowed, waiting for her to come through the door.

Hearing the click of the door knob, my heart is in my throat.

"Well, well, what do we have here?"

I don't move or look up at her.

"Why are you here?"

I stay silent.

"You may speak." She's slowly undressing. I can hear it, but I don't dare look up. She only told me to speak.

"I need you to get me back into shape. I felt something today, and I don't want to."

I can hear her walk toward me, but I remain still. My cock defies me, though, and is slowly getting hard. I feel her presence behind me. She grabs my head and tugs it back. I'm looking up toward the ceiling. Her breath is by my ear.

"For the whore you've been with behind my back?"

"Yes, Mistress."

"Did you think I didn't know?

"Yes, Mistress."

"So you want me to beat you?"

"Yes, Mistress."

"Why?"

Before I can answer her, she pushes my head back down forcefully before smacking me across the back of the head. She walks away, and I hear the belt slide out of the loops. The first smack lands across my back. I whimper, but immediately feel better at the sharp sting.

Once we've finished and I'm dressing, she sits on the bed staring at me.

"I don't have much news on Caston and Sabrina, but I should have information for you soon."

She shakes her head and waves me away.

Leaving Beverly's clutches, I'm still thinking about Kaitlyn. Her eyes are staring into my soul. Shit. I walk out of my condo and continue on to the park. I sit on a bench and stare off.

Letting my head fall back, I cover my face and scrub hard, fighting to wipe away the memories that want to surface.

Crash, bang, yelling. I hear him move through the house. I cower in the corner of my room, trying to be as quiet as I can be. He's drunk again. I hate it. Mom's working, so she won't know. Just like always.

"Mark, where are you, you little bastard?"

Pulling my legs tighter into me, I bend my head into knees.

Ric comes to door and wiggles the knob. I locked it. Big mistake. He kicks it open. Walking over to me, he picks me up by my hair and flings me onto the bed. I'm only six. I scramble to the headboard. He smacks me so hard this time my head flies into the headboard, and I pass out.

I wake up to my mom covering me and kissing my head. It hurts so badly, but I don't say anything. He always cleans up, so she has no idea what happens when she's at work. She doesn't realize I wasn't sleeping.

My stomach turns when he walks in behind her and places a kiss on her cheek. "Let him sleep, Ann. He's had a rough night." He ruffles my head and gives it a shove once she has already turned to leave the room.

Ric's always been good to Mom. He took us in when my dad died. Mom is head over heels for him, so I'm happy for her.

I'm sixteen, cocky, and untouchable at school. I'm the bully all the teachers love. No matter what I do, I never get in trouble. It's great. I'm in control—until I get home. Then he gets a hold of me again.

Having sex for the first time, it's so fast the girl laughs at me. I'm not sure what comes over me. Rage bubbles inside me, and I back hand her. Shocked she stares at me. I'm shocked. I've never hit anyone before. It feels strange. When she says I will pay, fear courses through me. I see red and hit her again.

After explaining to her she will keep quiet, I pull my pants up and leave her.

She never says anything. I get away with it. I have control.

I continue down that path through high school, and when I get a scholarship to State, I'm a god. No one could touch me.

I turn on the bench and punch it. "FUCK!" I scream.

Getting up, I sprint back to the condo, I jump in the car and drive back to the hotel.

I'm out of breath when I get to the door. She opens it with a surprised look.

"Mark, I didn't think I'd…"

I take her mouth forcefully as I walk her back into the room.

"I didn't think I'd be back here, Kaitlyn."

She smiles at me. "You know my name."

I kiss her again. All I want to do I strip her and claim her as mine.

My cell phone alert goes off, and I reach in my pocket to grab it. Cracking my eye open, I see it's a message from Bruce. He's a friend of mine that has an in with Terrance. I roll over to kiss Kaitlyn on the shoulder.

"I really have to get this, baby."

She just mumbles and pulls the covers up further to her neck.

Sliding out of bed, I grab my boxers and slide them on. I walk into the bathroom and shut the door. I dial Bruce back after I turn on the water to make sure Kaitlyn doesn't hear anything I say.

"Hey, man, what's up?"

"Where the fuck are you?"

"Don't fucking worry about it. What do you have for me?"

"Chill, bro. Terrance isn't as tight lipped as we thought. I was able to get him to hire me and last night I was even able to get into the house. Did you know about Caston's mom?"

"Beverly, ya, I know all about her."

"No, dude, not Beverly."

"What?" I sit down on the toilet.

"Ya, apparently Beverly is his aunt."

I'm shocked into silence while Bruce fills me in on the fucked up relationship between that family.

"This gives me a ton to work with, thanks, bud."

"Oh, that's not even the best part yet. Are you ready?"

Probably not, I think, but it's not like I can prevent it. I grow irritated waiting for him to continue.

"Fucking spit it out already. Do you think I enjoy talking to you when I could be in bed?"

"Hot piece of ass?"

"Fuck off, Bruce. Are you going to tell me, or not?"

"Okay, okay. Rose, Caston's real mom, who's dead—she's not, bro. She's alive and well."

"Fuck me. Thanks."

I quickly hang up and jump in the shower, so it at least seems like I wasn't on the phone for so long. Now, how do I use this information to my advantage?

Chapter Sixteen

Sabrina

It's been a few days since Caston's admitted to me that he wanted to meet Rose. He's been silent and a bit distant since that day. I'm worried. It's Saturday and instead of waking up in Caston's arms, warm and content, I'm waking up alone. He has snuck off again without waking me to say goodbye.

I swing my legs over the side of the bed and reach to the end, grabbing Caston's white dress shirt from last night. Feeling the cotton slide along my skin warms me on the inside. The smell of Caston on the shirt makes my insides flip flop.

Getting up slowly, I stretch. As I stretch, I see my dance shoes poking out from under the bed. I crouch down and pull them out. It's been so long. My heart starts racing as I hold them. The feeling of love that I used to feel dancing is coming back, but my heart aches, thinking about what the doctors have told me. Never again? I can't believe that. I can't. This is a part of me. I slide the shoes on and still crouched down I press one foot over onto pointe. My calf tightens. I stand flat footed and roll through my feet one at a time to remind my body what I want them to do.

I do a few pliés, roll my ankles, and point my toes. I don't feel strong enough to let go of the bed, but my body is listening to me. It's protesting slightly, but every little bit makes me stronger. I need this to feel whole again.

I'm so in tune with stretches I don't notice Caston had walked into the room until I turn around.

"Caston," I say breathless, slightly embarrassed to have him find me like this.

He's immediately in front of me, grabbing my face in his hands. His lips engulf mine. Before I can deepen the kiss he backs away and rests his forehead on mine.

"Bre, when I approached the door and saw you standing here in your pointe shoes, my heart just stopped. I couldn't believe my eyes. I've been waiting for…" He stops mid-sentence and kisses me again. A tear escapes my eye.

"I don't think I will ever be back where I was. I want to be back there, Cass, oh God do I want to be back there."

He wraps me in his arms and kisses my neck. "I want to show you something."

I back out of his embrace and nod. Caston grabs my hand and kisses it lightly as a smile crosses his face. The first I've seen in a few days. He leads me down the hall to the last door on the left. I wonder what's so special about this room. I've seen it before. It's just a spare bedroom.

"Close your eyes."

I giggle and shake my head. "You're crazy, Caston, I've already been in this room. What's so special about a spare room?"

He playfully scowls. "Will you just close your eyes, women?"

Laughing, I lean up and place a light kiss on his lips. "Okay, baby, don't get your boxers in a bunch."

I lean back and cover my eyes with my hand. Hearing the door open, I really want to peek. Caston takes my other hand and leads me into the room. It feels like I've been standing there forever.

He moves behind me and slides his arms around my waist, his chin rests on my shoulder.

"Can I open my eyes now?"

He places a kiss right below my ear. "Yes, open them," he whispers.

My hand drops and so does my jaw. The breath leaves my body, and my knees feel like they are about to give out on me. I'm standing in my very own dance studio. The furniture has been removed and mirrors are on one wall. There are bars opposite the mirrors and in the corner a state of the art sound system.

I'm speechless. I didn't know what to say.

"Do you like it?" Caston sounds worried and unsure. "I was waiting until I knew it was right to show you. When I walked in today and saw you standing there, I knew it was time."

"When, how?" Is all I could manage.

"The floor was already hardwood, so all I had to do was clear the room and add a few finishing touches. I talked to Professor Lee and got what she suggested. Do you like it, baby?"

I turn in his arms. "Caston, I love it, but I don't think I'll ever get to use it."

He tips my head back to look up at him. "Bre, I won't give up on you. Just seeing you standing there in my shirt and your dance shoes made me realize you won't let anything hold you back. No doctors, no leg muscles. You *will* dance again."

Tears roll down my face. "How do you have so much faith?"

"Because you won't let anything stand in your way."

I bury my head in his chest and take a deep breath. He's right. He usually is. I feel so empowered just standing here in my shoes. I needed this.

"I've been watching you, Bre. You've been getting so strong. You hardly have a limp anymore, and it's only been a few months. It's unreal how far you've come from the day I told you what the doctors said. It still kills me I had to tell you that. I'm so sorry."

"Stop it." I step out of his arms, making him look at me. I hate when he blames himself. "It was not your fault, Caston." He looks away. "Look at me, damn it."

His eyes meet mine. I back away a little more. "This," I pull up his shirt to show my scar, "is not your fault. Beverly is a sick, twisted bitch, but she can't get to us anymore. I want you to stop blaming yourself. I'm embracing it. I need you to as well."

He takes a deep breath. "God, you have no idea how sexy you are right now, Sabrina."

"Don't change the subject, Caston."

His sexy lopsided smile creeps onto his face, and I melt. Damn it, he knows my weakness.

"I'm not, Sabrina. I'm embracing it." He reaches down and grabs his hard cock straining in his pants.

I shake my head and let a laugh escape. "You're bad." Turning to walk toward the sound system, Caston is immediately behind me, pulling me back to him.

"Am I, Ms. Bennett?" He turns me toward the mirror, and I catch his eyes. The bright blues are hooded. Brushing my hair to the side, he places a few kisses and a nip on my neck, making every nerve endings come alive.

"Look at yourself in the mirror," he commands.

His white shirt hangs to my knees. I'm dwarfed in it, but he's right; I don't think I've ever looked sexier, but I think it could be the constant flush on my face when I'm around Caston.

His arms reach around and slowly he starts to unbutton the shirt, keeping his eyes locked on mine. Once it's open, he slowly pulls it down my shoulders and lets it fall to the floor. His hands slide up my arms. Reaching my shoulders, he rubs small circles before sliding his hands down the front of me, cupping my breasts and rolling my nipples between his fingers.

"Oh, Caston." My head falls back onto his shoulder.

"Bre, I said to look at yourself in the mirror." My eyes catch his again. "Do you know how sexy you look standing here?"

I shake my head, and he places a few kisses on my shoulder.

"Let me tell you." His voice is smooth and sultry. It sends a shiver down my spine.

I look at him as his eyes rake up and down my body. Just as I'm about to move to cover myself, his hands move down and rest on my hips, creating a tingling trail where his hands have been.

He places a kiss behind my ear. "Where should I start, love?"

I take a deep breath and a moan rumbles through my body.

"Your eyes are soulful. The most sparkling hazel gems I've ever seen. If I could find a stone that depicts what I see when I look into your eyes, I would make millions. Anyone that meets you can see how genuine and beautiful you are on the inside and out just by gazing into your eyes."

His right hand traces a line along my jaw as he continues. "Your lips. Your lips are perfect. Not too thin, not too plump, a perfect heart. Your lips are soft and inviting. I especially love to see them wrapped around my cock. They were made for me." I feel him become even harder behind me.

Exasperated, I smile and say, "Caston."

He continues without skipping a beat. "I love to see your smile first thing in the morning, it lights up my day, and it's the thing I love to see right before my eyes close for the night. You complete my day. I love to watch when you meet someone for the first time and they see your smile. You brighten a room, and people flock to you just from your smile."

Both of his hands move and gather my hair into a ponytail before wrapping it around his hand. "Your hair is natural. I love that you haven't altered it like so many women do nowadays. It's silky and the perfect length." He tugs it down, making me adjust my head up and over to the side, giving him better access to my neck. "I can make you turn and do this." His mouth connects with my hot skin. I moan and close my eyes. I can feel the suction and the slight nips of his teeth on my skin. I'm going to have a mark, but right now my insides are clenching, and I don't give a shit.

My breathing increases as I wonder where he's going to go next. I'm speechless, listening to him worship my body.

His hands slide from my shoulders down to my hands. He intertwines our fingers and pulls my arms up and out into a T. As he lets go of my hands, he lightly strokes my skin back and forth, making it pebble with goose bumps. "Your arms are perfect—not too muscular, not too skinny. Perfect. I especially love them wrapped around me when you hug me. Your hands fit perfectly in mine. I love the way they feel when I'm holding them, so petite and delicate."

His hands engulf mine, and I love it. It makes me feel safe. Just as I'm thinking about it he brings my hands up to his lips and lightly brushes a kiss on the back of each hand.

"Caston—"

"Shhh, no talking. I'm telling you how beautiful and sexy you are." His smile is so devilish I blush.

Chapter Seventeen

Caston

Seeing the blush creep across her body puts my body on high alert. She's so damn sexy and she has no idea. I'm so hard, I'm in pain. I want nothing more than to lift her up and fuck her up against the wall right now, but I need to finish worshiping her body.

"Are you wet, baby?"

Her eyes are glazed over and a small hum comes from her lips. That little noise makes me want her even more.

"Shall I continue?"

Her eyes catch mine again in the mirror, and she nods slowly.

I lower her hands to her sides and run my hands back up her body and move them to the front of her. I cup her breasts, letting the weight of her mounds rest in my palms. "Your breasts are perfect. Just the right size to fill my hands. Just enough to give you gorgeous cleavage, but not too much that you can't go braless. Fuck, I love these so much." I let out a small grunt when I move my hands to tweak her nipples. "Damn, Bre, you are so responsive to my touch. Your nipples are so inviting."

I remove my hands from her breast, and I hear a whimper from the loss of my touch. I smirk knowing how much she loves it.

One hand lightly brushes the skin on her stomach. Watching her follow my hand along her skin makes me lick my lips. I want my mouth on her skin, I need to taste her. Moving in front of her, I kneel and place my hands on her hips. My left thumb falls over her Tinkerbelle tattoo, the one and only mark on her skin before the accident. "I love this." I place a kiss on it. So innocent.

"Caston," she groans, "God this is torture. I need you."

"I'm not done." I smirk up at her. Seeing her squirm is driving me over edge.

Kissing her tattoo again, I begin to move my lips along an invisible line to her other hip. I can feel her skin ripple under my lips. Letting my hands grace the length of her legs, I lean my head back to look at her.

"Your legs are sexy." I see her teeth clench and know she's about to argue with me.

"Don't," I warn.

She swallows hard and looks away. Her eyes are misty.

"I'm fucking serious, Sabrina. Your legs are beautiful. Long and sleek. When you would dance, you'd have the whole place watching you. Unbelievably strong, even your injured leg. I love kissing your legs, but I love having them wrapped around my waist even more. God, Bre." I kiss each leg multiple times.

"Last, but not least, this." I softly place a kiss on her pussy. Silky smooth, just the way I love it. "This, my dear, is the sexiest pussy I have ever seen." I lick her, letting my tongue dip in to taste her juices. I grip her hips and dive in to taste her again. She begins to shudder and her moans grew louder. Her hands grip my hair, pulling it harder than she ever has before.

"Caston, what are you doing to me?"

I just hum against her sensitive flesh, which makes her lose control. I feel a rush of liquid coat my tongue. Her knees start to give out from her orgasm. Helping her sink to the floor safely, I pull her into my lap, cradling her while she comes down from her high. She nuzzles her head into my neck. I let my hand rub up and down her leg, letting her calm.

I feel tears fall onto my chest. "Hey, hey, no tears. Why are you crying?"

My hand happens to stop on her scar, immediately I feel her stiffen in my arms. Tilting her head up to look at me, I place a chaste kiss on her lips.

"Don't do that, Bre. I want to see the fire in your eyes that I just saw in the bedroom when you didn't know I was watching. I want to see the same light I saw when I was telling you how beautiful you are."

She wipes her eyes with the back of her hands and sniffles, which makes me laugh. Cradling my face between her hands, she looks deep into my eyes and nods. The feeling that causes a smile to split my face in half is wonderful. She finally gets it.

Her eyes are seductive, and she kisses me while moving to straddle my lap. I let my hands trace the outline of her body. Knowing she still has her dance shoes on while she's naked makes me harder than ever. She feels it and grinds her sweet pussy into my lap, making me moan into her mouth.

I pull back a little. I don't want to stop, but this isn't the right place. She looks at me confused.

"I want nothing more than to take you right here, but it wouldn't be right. I need you to do something for me."

Her eyes widen, and she tentatively asks, "What's that?"

"I need you to dance for me."

She scrambles to get off of my lap. My heart breaks to see the look of defeat in her eye.

"Caston, I can't. You know I'm not strong enough."

She turns to grab the shirt she was wearing and proceeds to put it back on. Standing about five feet from me, she looks down at me with a mist in her eyes again. I crawl over to her, so she has to look down at me. The brown waves fall over her shoulders, framing her face. I sit at her feet, letting my hands stroke her calves.

"You can."

Her head shakes violently.

"Yes, Bre, you can."

I move my fingers to her right foot and undo the ribbons on her shoes. She isn't strong enough for her pointe shoes, but I know she can dance barefoot. She watches me move from one foot to the other. When I'm done, I slowly ease her feet off the ground one at a time and slip the shoes off, dropping them to the floor beside me. Bending over, I lightly kiss the top of each foot. Her breath hitches as I do this.

"Bre," I look up at her, "dance for me."

She's breathing hard by the rise and fall of her chest under my shirt. My breath stops, am I pushing too much? Finally, she nods very slowly as she turns to walk to the stereo in the corner. Pushing my hands through my hair, I let out the breath I was holding. I get up and walk to the chair in the corner of the room and wait.

She slowly walks to the stereo. Shaking her arms out and rolling her head on her shoulders. Her head does fall back, and she stands still, staring at the ceiling. I think she really wants to run out of the room, but she doesn't. She reaches for the iPad attached to the system and runs through the extensive music library.

I know it won't be an extreme dance or one that I've seen her do in the past. Just that she's willing to try makes me so fucking proud of her.

I hear a guitar start strumming, and I know exactly what song it is. My heart starts to beat wildly. She walks to the middle of the room and looks at me when the words of the song start. It's a perfect choice, "When You Say Nothing At All" by Allison Kraus.

Her movements are slow and calculated, but still so fluid and graceful. Not as much footwork, but what she does is breathtaking. She's in a zone. I can tell she isn't even seeing me anymore, it's just her and the music. Even though I can see her leg strain with certain moves, she keeps going. I never expected her to be this good so soon after the shooting. I feel myself choke up. The song starts to fade, and I slowly make my way over to her. She stops when I'm right in front of her, breathing heavily, with her arms wrapped around herself and her head hanging.

Her shoulders are slumped over and shaking. She's crying.

"You did it, Bre."

She looks up at me with a huge smile on her face and wraps her hands around my neck. I instantly pick her up, wrapping her legs around my waist.

"You did it."

She's sobbing, but I know it's a good cry this time.

"I'm so proud of you, baby. So fucking proud. You did it. I knew you could."

She hugs me harder than I thought she could. Her mouth crashes onto mine.

"Thank you," she says between kisses, "thank you for believing in me."

I walk her back to our room and place her on our bed. Slowly undressing, I take in the beautiful women in front of me. Crawling up her body, I place kisses along the way. She's mine to worship now, and I plan to do it slow and right.

Chapter Eighteen

Caston

Today's the day. Sabrina shifts nervously by my side as we make our way to Rose's house. After Sabrina danced, and I worshiped her again, she quietly confronted me about what had me so withdrawn. It felt like a weight was lifted off of me as she helped me understand how my mom could be so afraid. Bre had the experience with Mark to draw from. She said she could imagine how much worse it had been for Rose.

With a different perspective came the possibility of understanding and forgiveness. I called James and asked about meeting Rose, if she would be willing to meet me at this point. It didn't take him long to get back to me. Rose wanted to see me, but was still extremely fearful of coming back to town. So Bre and I agreed to travel to Rose's home.

I grab Bre's hand and pull it toward me. "Thank you for coming."

"I wouldn't have it any other way. We're in this together."

My mind wonders, thinking about what my life could have been if all this shit never happened. Would I have even met Sabrina, would I still have my businesses, hell, would I even be alive? I don't even know what I want to say to them. I've been going over and over it in my head but nothing seems to be right.

"Stop overthinking," she says, reading my mind.

I glance over at her. "How do you do that?"

"Do what?"

"Know exactly what to say."

Shaking her head, she glances out the side window. "We're connected."

I couldn't disagree. Knowing something was on her mind too, I contemplated asking her.

"Bre, I don't know what's going to happen today. I'm not sure what I'm going to do."

She reassuringly squeezed my hand. "I support you one hundred percent no matter what you decide."

We pull up to a house miles away from anyone else. After a few moments, I get out and walk around to open her door. She swings her long legs out, and I can see a hint of skin just above her stockings. She moves to stand up with the help of my outstretched hand. It's very quiet.

Closing the door behind her, I lock it. The noise echoes through the silence.

"Why do I feel like we're in the beginning of a horror movie?" she asked.

I laugh deep. "Does have that feel to it, doesn't it?"

Sliding my hand around her waist, I walk her to the front door. The door is opened by a kind-looking lady. She greets us with a warm smile.

"Welcome. You must be Caston, and you must be Bre. Pictures don't do the two of you justice." She steps back and extends her arm into the entryway. "Please, come in. Rose and James—your mom and dad are in the garden. It's Rose's pride and joy, well, next to you." She smiles at Caston as she walks. "Dr. Sebastian would like a brief word with you before you talk to Rose."

As we enter a small living room, I notice another woman standing by a chair in front of the fireplace. Then next thing I notice are all of the pictures of me; snapshots, school photos, me standing in front of Rose Builders. So many photos. The doctor must notice my stunned expression.

"Yes, Rose, is quite proud of you. She keeps up with everything you are doing. James has been sure to keep her well informed on the man behind the public image." She holds her hand out to me. I'm still so caught up in everything around me my mind is blank. Thankfully Bre steps forward to shake her hand.

"Hello, Dr. Sebastian. I'm Sabrina, Caston's fiancée. You'll have to forgive him for a moment. This is all very overwhelming."

Dr. Sebastian gives me a reassuring smile. "I'm sure this has been quite a lot to deal with, which is why I wanted to speak with you before you meet with Rose. Have a seat, please. I won't keep you long. I know you're anxious to proceed."

Bre clasps my hand, drawing me over to the couch as Dr. Sebastian took her seat. I tighten my grip on Sabrina's hand as the doctor begins to speak again.

"First of all, I want to thank you for coming to see Rose. This is a tremendous step for her. I've been her therapist since almost immediately after she was found. I know you must have a lot of conflicting feelings about everything that you've been told. I understand this is very confusing for you. I know how much Rose loves you. Her fear for you is very deep seeded. James told me he forwarded her file to you." I grimace and can practically feel my body shudder at the memories contained in that file. "Yes, Caston, it is disturbing to read. Consider how it would be to live with that in your mind. Rose lived in a mental prison for years after her escape. It has taken years to get her to this point, and she is still very fragile emotionally. I see her agreeing to meet you as a giant step forward for her. We are all hopeful that seeing you in person, seeing that you are alive and thriving, will help her let go of the fear and begin to live a fuller life. Before you meet Rose, do you have any questions for me?"

I say the first thing to pop into my mind, "Could meeting me be detrimental to my mom?" I barely get the words past the huge lump in my throat.

"Caston, I'll be honest, we really don't know. But Rose seems ready, and she's cautiously excited to see you. Besides the fear she has for your safety, she's afraid you will reject her because of what happened to her?"

"No… it's just all so very confusing, Dr. Sebastian. I don't know where to begin…" Letting my statement drift off.

"That's okay. Being confused is normal. I'll be here to help both of you through this. There's still a lot of healing to be done. And, please, call me Nancy. We'll all work together as a team." Nancy says with a confident tone that causes me to nod my head.

"Now, would you like to go meet your mom?"

We walk down the hall hand in hand. I'm doing my best to stay calm and strong for Sabrina, but damn it's hard because I'm a ball of nerves right now.

Reaching the French doors leading to the garden, I draw a deep breath. I'm fighting to control my racing hearting. I feel like I could hyperventilate. My feet suddenly feel like blocks of lead.

"Caston." My name pulls me from the verge of a panic attack. "I'll be here with you. We can leave any time. You tell me the moment you are ready." I squeeze her hand and step forward.

"Wow," Bre says breathlessly, "it's like a Kincaid painting. Come to think of it, the whole house is like that, eerily perfect." I chuckle and slowly follow the brick path.

After a couple of hundred feet there's a break in the flowers. There's a small clearing with a fountain in the center with a wooden swing to the right and a gazebo to the left.

James is sitting at the table, gazing across the courtyard. Following his gaze, I spot the small woman kneeling in front of a Camellia bush. She appears to be gardening. Once again, I'm unsure of what to do. This is a very foreign feeling for me. James must sense our presence because he stands up and speaks softly as he walks towards the woman… my mom.

"Rose, they're here." She freezes. You can see her start to tremble. When James reaches her side, he kneels down and soothes her by speaking quietly to her. She nods her head and takes a deep breath.

James stands and extends his hand to help her up. He wraps an arm around her shoulders, and she seems to cling to him for security. She still hasn't looked up. Finally, when they're about ten feet from us she raises her gaze to meet mine. She gasp and tears fill her eyes. "Oh my, you're so tall. I worried you would take after me, instead of James."

I release the breath I had been holding with a little laugh at such an odd thing to say to the child you haven't seen in twenty-two years.

I look her over from head to toe. She's so small. Her eyes don't shine like they did the last time I saw her. Sabrina's hand tightens on mine, and I know I need to say something back.

"Mom, I'm sorry."

She wrings her hands in front of her and holds her head down. Shaking it back and forth. James walks her toward the gazebo away from me.

"Did I say something wrong?" I look toward Nancy for clarification.

She places a hand on my forearm. "No, just give her a minute."

Walking toward the gazebo James looks up and smiles. I suddenly get the urge to protect her. "She's okay now," he says.

Now that we're all seated in the gazebo, it's too quiet. I really don't know what to say without scaring her. Then I figure it out. This garden, her pride and joy. "Mom," I say quietly, "you have a beautiful garden. Will you tell me about it?"

Her eyes hesitantly meet mine, lighting up, and the smile that spreads onto her face makes my heart melt. I remember this Rose. Talking about the garden provides a peek at her old self. Her words start fast, and her hands are animated explaining the different plants she has and why those grow the best. Sabrina squeezes my thigh, and I know it's because she's as excited as I am to see Rose relax and engage with us. She's been talking for almost a half hour straight when she suddenly stops. Her hands fly to her mouth. "Oh dear me, I've just been rambling on. I'm sorry."

Nancy reaches over and pats her leg. "It's okay, Rose. You're doing good."

Rose's eyes fall to the ground, and she sticks her hands in her lap. I want nothing more than to hear her talk again. "Mom?" She doesn't look up, but instead curls into James's side. "Rose, will you show me some of your favorite plants?"

Nancy looks over to me with her eyes wide. Did I do something wrong? Then suddenly Rose gets up and walks over to me. She cautiously holds her hand out to me. I look over at Sabrina to see if this is really happening. The tears trailing down Bre's face confirm that my mom, the frightened shell, is reaching out to me. Quickly taking it, I follow her down the path and toward the back of the garden.

We walk away in silence, hand in hand, just like when I was little. Memories come flooding back to me of my life with her and how happy I was. My heart flutters, and I just want to pull her into a hug, but I know that would scare her away. When we finally reach the back of the garden, she stops. We are standing in front of a wall of rose bushes that are covered in blooms of every shade.

"Wow, these are beautiful." I whisper.

"Caston, I'm sorry."

I was taken back. "Mom, I know—I know what you've been through, all of it. You have nothing to be sorry for."

She looks up into my eyes. Her eyes are brimming with tears that fall in a steady stream down a face so different from the one I remember, yet the same. "I should have been there for you. I should have protected you. I let you down."

"Please, don't say that." A few weeks ago my response would have been different, but now I just want her to get better. "Everything is going to be okay."

She nods and looks back over to the bushes, pulling away from me mentally again.

"May I pick a rose to take back to Sabrina?"

Her gaze comes back to me, and she smiles before reaching forward and snapping off the most beautiful bud off the bush in front of us.

"I'm so happy to see you've grown into an amazing man. Just like your dad." I have to grit my teeth thinking of him leaving me with Beverly. "Caston," she reaches up and cups my cheek, "don't be mad at him. He was only doing what I asked. James tried on many occasions to get me to allow you to visit. But I—I was too afraid. I thought that Beverly had what she wanted when she got you and James. I desperately wanted to believe that you were being loved and cared for. You always seemed so happy in your pictures." She shakes her head as if trying to erase the doubts that have taken residence in her mind and turns to walk back to the others.

We head back to the gazebo in silence, and I twirl the rose between my fingers. When we get back, she stands at the entrance. "James, I'd like to take a nap. Can I please go lie down?"

My heart sinks. She doesn't want to be with me anymore. Nodding he gets up to rush to her side and whisks her off into the house.

"That's it?" I ask Nancy, a little frustrated.

"For today. This was a huge step for her. I was shocked she went with you by herself. Caston do you know how big that was? I feel she will start to come around. Please, say you will come back soon."

Sabrina joins me and links her arm with mine as Nancy ushers us out the door. I thank her for all her help. Once at the car, I pull Sabrina into a hug. I want to feel love flow through me, and I know I'll feel it with Bre. She doesn't ask me what happened, she knows I will tell her when I'm ready, and I'm thankful for the way she understands me.

The next morning, we settle into the drive back home after our flight back, I watch her check her phone more than once. I can see her grit her teeth. "What's wrong?" I ask.

"Oh, nothing. In that short time, I have twenty emails from Sara, Beth, and Rocco."

"Rocco?" My head snaps to her.

"The wedding coordinator. Remember?" She laughs.

"Oh yes, we'd like the chipper chicken." I try my best to quote the movie *Father of the Bride*.

"Caston." She rolls her eyes at me.

We fall into silence again.

"Are you okay with what happened?" Her voice is full of concern.

I grip the steering wheel and think about what she just asked. "Yeah. I mean, I was shocked to find out she was still alive. Then I was mad they could be so selfish. But once I got over being mad and really looked at her situation, I could understand. I can't comprehend what she endured. But I'm 'cautiously excited' to get to know her... and maybe have a real mom again." Looking over to her I grab her hand and squeeze it. "Thank you for coming with me."

"I wouldn't have it any other way."

As we get closer to town, my stomach rumbles.

"Getting hungry?" I question her.

Once again checking her phone, she sighs. "I'm up for anything that gets me out of answering these emails and texts. I just didn't think it'd be so crazy."

I belly laugh. "Bre, you decided to get married with a big wedding in two months."

She sticks her tongue out at me, but begins laughing.

Pulling into a nice Italian restaurant, I step out into the cool night air. Taking in the smell of garlic, I walk to Sabrina's side help her out, but before she can start moving, I pull her into my embrace.

"I love you."

Her hazel eyes meet mine, and she melts into my embrace. "I love you. That makes all this crazy worth it."

Holding her hand, we walk into the restaurant and get seated at a corner table with a view of the open kitchen.

"I love watching them cook all this stuff," she says in awe.

Her face lights up when they do some sort of fire on the grill. I place a wine and appetizer order with the waitress. Turning my attention back to Sabrina, I'm lost watching her expressions.

Suddenly, there is a commotion behind Sabrina. That's when I see her. Beverly.

"Son of a bitch," I mutter under my breath.

Sensing what's happening, Sabrina immediately goes pale.

I stand up and place a hand on her shoulder. She covers it with her hand. "I'll take care of this, Bre. Stay here, okay."

She nods, but I can see the worry on her face.

Quickly I take off for the front of the building. Informing the manager of the problem we have, I stay off to the side as he walks over to her table and leans down to speak in her ear. She looks over at him. I can almost see the anger rolling off her shoulders.

She stands up and looks around the restaurant. I immediately tense. I hope she doesn't see Sabrina. Knowing this isn't going to end well, I call Detective Alverez.

Before she can make it to Bre, I intercept her. "Beverly, let's not cause a scene." I hold my hands out in front of me, stopping her in her path.

"Caston, dear. I was just going to say hello."

Her voice is fake, and it sends a shiver down my spine.

"You know you are in violation of your restraining order." I try to stay as calm as I can. She could snap at any time.

She places her hands on her hips. "That's a funny thing, isn't it? Why do I have to be the one to leave? I was obviously here before you. My food is on the table. Funny the way the judicial system is, right?"

Her laugh echoes off the walls that feel like they are closing in on us. I keep her talking as calm as I can until I see Detective Alverez walk through the door. Immediately walking up to us, he grabs her hands, pulling them behind her back, placing cuffs on her.

"Beverly Holden, you are under arrest for not following the orders of the restraining orders Mr. Black and Ms. Bennett have against you. Anything you say, can and will be used against you in the court of law…" he speaks while dragging her out of the building.

The commotion in the restaurant is high. People are whispering and taking pictures on their phone. I shake my head, walking back to Sabrina. Taking my seat, I call the manager over.

"Please, let me pay for everyone in the restaurant now. I'm sorry for the inconvenience and the outburst that just happened. I feel bad for ruining their dinners."

"That is not necessary, sir," he tries to argue.

"I insist."

He nods his understanding and walks away.

Sabrina smiles at me, holding her hands out over the table for me to grab. I take them and place a kiss on each palm before entwining our fingers.

"She's going back to jail. Hopefully, she will be held until the trial. Now, where were we?"

"Just like that?" she asks, her face full of concern.

"Just like that," I respond.

Chapter Nineteen

Sabrina

It's only been two weeks since I decided I wanted a quick wedding. Never in my life did I anticipate the crazy train I'd departed on. Thankfully, Sara was able to get the top wedding planner, and it just happened to work out that the church and reception site that was the 'it' place were both free. I was reluctant at first. Originally, I wanted a nice quiet wedding in our backyard, but somehow I got Beth and Sara to talk me into the big fairytale. They insisted I'd be sorry. I gave in, and they were right in some respects, what little girl doesn't dream of their wedding day? Mine was always to a prince charming, which I've found, and me wearing a big poofy dress in a church. Now, however, with every passing email and decision my nerves are strung tighter. I still wasn't feeling well, even with the change of medicine, but the doctor assured me it was just the nerves. She also said that if I didn't relax, I'd have an ulcer in no time. The news is all over us about the incident with Beverly, and now they are focusing on the so called 'wedding of the year'. Everyone has been trying to find out when it would be, where we would have it, and every time we went out, they bombarded us with questions trying to find out anything they could. Relentless vultures. I just want this to be over; I'm kind of wishing I'd taken Caston up on eloping last week when I was stressing over cake flavors.

I make it into the office and sit at my desk, hoping to clear my head. My email pings, and I sigh. I wonder what I'll have to decide on today. Just as I'm about to pull up the awaiting email, Sara pops her head in.

"Hey, got a minute."

I check the time and see I have about twenty minutes before the photo shoot today.

"Come on in. If you ask me anything about wedding decisions, I think I might call security on you."

She chuckles as she slowly moves the notebook behind her back.

"Why so gloomy?" Her concerned look contrasts her bright and cheery blue suit with black tights and black heels.

I open a drawer in my desk and pull out a bottle of water. "Just not feeling well."

"Still?" She moves over to me and places her hand on my head.

I shrug her off. "My nerves are just shot with this wedding crap."

"Understandable."

She moves to sit on the couch by my desk, and I get up to follow her.

"Before I start," Sara grabs my hands and smiles, "if anything gets too much just let me know, I'll shut up."

I smile back at her, my stomach flips at her touch. Taking a deep breath in, I blow it out and nod.

"Okay, since our bridal party spa day was last week and the wedding is only six weeks away let's discuss the bachelorette party."

I let out a huge laugh. "And here I thought this was going to be a serious conversation."

Just then the door to my office opens, and Beth pops in. "What's up, bitches?" she exclaims, stepping into the office.

A huge smile breaks on my face, and I look over at Sara in disbelief. She's laughing. I jump up and squeal.

"BETH! You're here! Oh my God!"

She runs toward me, and we jump up and down laughing. I thought Beth was out of town for business, and she shows up here. I'm in disbelief. As she was talking a mile a minute about how Sara contacted her and how excited she is about their surprise for me, Caston walks into the room with a cocky smirk on his face.

"You knew about Beth being in town?" I rush to his arms while lightly smacking him on the chest.

He plays hurt before swooping me up in a big bear hug. "Of course I did, Bre." Then he plants a sloppy kiss on my cheek. "I knew everyone was here when I heard shrieking across the entire building."

Sara walks up next to us. "Bre, Beth and I are going to take you away for a nice relaxing girl's weekend."

My stomach drops. It sounds wonderful, but being away from Caston makes me nervous. I'm not sure why. I try to fake a smile, but Caston sees right through me and squeezes my waist. He leans over to kiss my cheek again and whispers in my ear, "It's only for a couple of days."

Sara and Beth link arms, smiling at me like kids in a candy shop. "We leave in an hour," Beth chimes in.

My eyes go wide, an hour. "But my photo shoot," I grasp for an excuse to procrastinate.

"I've got you covered already," Caston says. "I was in charge before you got here, remember?"

I let out a nervous laugh and turn my head to his chest, taking a deep breath. I love his smell. Caston's thumb strokes my back. I look up into his eyes, but talk to the girls, "Well, I guess I need to pack then."

He leans over and kisses my nose.

"Let me just check my email before I—"

"No, no emails and no packing, the girls already took care of that this morning after you left." Caston spins me around and pushes me into the hall with Sara and Beth following us out the door.

Before the girls join us, I jump into Caston's arms and plant a large kiss on him. Hoots and hollers fill the hall behind us. Not only from the girls, but from some of the employees as well.

Separating from him, I rest my forehead on his.

"Bre, if you don't stop, I'm going to have to take you into that supply closet and have my way with you."

I look down at him with a devilish grin. Before I can take him up on the offer, Sara comes up behind Caston and tickles him, making him move quickly to set me down. Beth races up and starts to drag me away laughing.

"I'll take you up on that offer next time," I yell as I continue down the hall. "I love you, Caston."

"Love you more, Sabrina."

His smiling face is the last thing I see before I get into the limo.

Beth is the last one in and, once she's seated, she pops the cork on the champagne. A small squeal escapes us. Pouring a round of bubbly into our glasses, Sara gives me a quick hug.

"Let's toast." Sara says.

She places her free arm around my shoulder, and Beth places her hand on my knee, squeezing it.

"To Sabrina and Caston, may their life together continue to be sexy, spontaneous, and fulfilling. To putting the past behind them and moving on stronger."

We clink glasses. It gets quiet in the limo. I sigh.

"Okay, that was a mood killer, huh?"

Sara and I just laugh.

"Let's try this again." Beth refills our glasses and continues. "To Sabrina. May her life be filled with an unlimited amount of sex, earth shattering orgasms, and may it never get dull or lifeless. May our weekend be crazy, and remember what happens on the trip stays on the trip."

"Woooooooooo Hooooooooooo!" Sara squeals, and we all laugh, drinking the next glass of champagne.

After a little gossip about the club my curiosity is getting the better of me.

"Where are we going?" I laugh.

"Nope, not telling you," Beth says. Sara and she exchange a glance.

My eyebrow arches. "What do you two have planned? I'm afraid."

My email pings on my phone again. I reach into my purse to check it, but Sara intercepts it and steals my phone.

"But, work. You just pulled me out without being able to put the out of office notification on my email or close up my work."

She shakes her head. "First rule, no cell phones. This is a girls' weekend only."

I cross my arms over my chest, like a pouting three year old. My nerves are already shot and this isn't what I need.

"Please, just let me call Caston and my assistant to get everything taken care of, then I promise you can take my phone." Pausing before I make any rash promises, I ask, "Do I at least get it at night?"

They share glances, unspoken words pass between them. I can tell they've already had decided they weren't going to let me. Just when I think I'm going to lose this battle, Beth turns to me and holds up her hand.

"Okay, one call. Decide, Caston or your assistant, not both. Then we get your phone. I'm not promising you'll get your phone at night. We don't want you thinking about any wedding stuff this weekend."

I clap my hands, since I got my way. Grabbing the phone from Sara's grasp, I playfully stick my tongue at her.

Sara grabs my hand before I can dial and pulls me into her. I quickly glance at Beth because she isn't aware of how close Sara and I really are, but thankfully she's not looking because she's playing with the stereo.

Looking back at Sara she leans in to my ear and whispers, "Better watch that tongue, or I'll put it to better use."

My breath catches in my throat, and I swallow hard. She backs away and moves to help Beth with the music, leaving me some privacy to make my call.

I take a few deep breaths to calm myself before I dial Caston.

"Sabrina, what's wrong?" he answers on the first ring.

"Nothing. I need you to do a few things for me that I didn't get to do before I was rushed out of my office."

"My God, baby, I was worried. Sara and Beth told me the no cell phone rule, so having you call scared the living daylights out of me. Thank God you're okay."

I scoot closer to the window to try to get more privacy. "I'm fine, not happy about the no phone rule, but excited to get away."

Hearing him chuckle makes me smile. I love that sound.

"So, can you do a few things for me?"

"Of course, baby, what do you need?"

"Okay, can you please set my out of office on my email?"

"Of course, I can. I'll have my assistant do that right away."

I hear him shuffle some papers around.

"Caston, I need you to do it. Please? I'm only given one call, like I'm in prison, and I want you to do it personally." I happen to pull out my whiny, sing song voice that gets him every time.

"Sabrina, you know you don't have to beg, but I sure like when you do."

I smile and glance out the window. "You do? What does it do to you?"

"Oh Sabrina," the words are more of a plea, "you have no idea."

Beth slugs me on the shoulder to get my attention. "Ouch!"

"Time's up, Bre."

"No."

Sara responds, "Oh yes, plus we don't want to hear phone sex between you and Caston."

Hearing the girls, Caston starts laughing. "I'll let you go, babe. If they give you the phone back, call me and we can do it right."

"Fuck." I let my head fall back onto the seat. "Damn it, Caston, now I'm horny."

This sends the girls into a fit of laughter.

"Go, have fun, be safe, and I'll take care of everything. Personally."

A smile splits my face. "Thank you, honey. I love you."

"Love you too, Bre, more than you will ever know."

I hang up my phone and unwillingly hand it over to Sara.

"Okay, I'm all yours. Do whatever you want to me." I hold my hands up in surrender with a huge smile on my face.

I may pretend that I'm upset about this impromptu trip, but I'm only trying to put up a tough exterior. I'm jumping up and down on the inside.

Beth pulls some cheesy bachelorette items from her purse and places them on me. I'm now decked out in a plastic tiara, sash, and light up ribbons pinned to my shirt.

Before they can do anything, else we pull up to the airport and Caston's private jet is sitting on the tarmac waiting for us. I turn to them with eyes wide.

"Okay, spill it. You know I hate flying."

We step out of the limo, and the stewardess greets us.

"Welcome, ladies. The flight looks like it will be a smooth one and the masseurs will be set up in the bedroom once we hit cruising altitude."

"Eeeek!" Beth bounds up the steps, leaving Sara and I behind. "Come on slow pokes!"

Sara holds out her hand to me. I place my hand in hers, and we walk up the steps together.

They still haven't told me where we are going. "Before I go any further, I want to know where we are going."

"Don't worry, Sabrina, it's Caston approved," Sara teases.

"Should we just tell her?" Beth asks as she sets her purse down.

"Yes!" I demand.

"Damn, Bre. When did you get so demanding?" Beth walks up to me and puts her hands on my shoulders.

I just glare at her.

"Okay, fine. We're going to Caston's house in Mexico."

My mouth falls open.

Sara interrupts, "Riveria Maya, Mexico to be specific. It's around Cancun. He has a villa on the beach. It's fully staffed, so it's kind of like our own personal resort."

I blink a few times with my mouth still hanging open.

Laughing Sara and Beth, link arms with me. "Okay, I think we have officially shocked her. Let's get this party started." Once the pilot announces we can move about the cabin, they lead me back to the bedroom where three really muscular, tan men are setting up massage tables for us. I'm sure they weren't Caston approved.

Sara gasps at the sight of the men. "Holy shit, this is going to be a weekend for the record books."

Chapter Twenty

Caston

I wave goodbye to Sabrina and the girls before turning to head back to my office. Laughing on my way up, I can only imagine what Sara and Beth have up their sleeves. Maybe it's better that I don't think about it.

After Bre's brief phone call, I pour myself into work. Anything to keep my mind off of Sabrina. I know that I won't hear from her for a few days because Sara's taking her phone hostage. Back to back meetings, a few model scouting portfolios, and the work day is done. Clearing off my desk, I stand to the leave when I remember what Bre asked me to do.

I walk to the other side of the building and into her office. All the lights were on and she did, in fact, leave the computer on. Laughing to myself as I look over her desk of organized chaos, I pull up her email.

I'm dumbfounded when I see three emails from Broc today. Wondering how often she talks to Broc, I sort her emails by sender. I'm relieved to see these were the only ones. Wondering why he emailed her today, I open the first one up.

Sabrina—

I wanted you to know that I'm worried Mark is up to something. Please call me. Same number as always.

Broc

My heart starts racing. No, this can't be happening. I click the next one.

Sabrina—

I know I just sent you an email, but I was worried that you are just ignoring me. Please call me.

Broc

I call Terrance, informing him that as soon as the plane is back from dropping off the girls, I want it refueled and ready to head back. Clicking open the next email, I paraphrase the emails to him, so he knows what's going on.

Sabrina—

He's been at Beth's apartment. Please.

Broc

The phone rings three times. I'm chewing on my thumb and tapping my heel on the ground, willing him to answer his phone.

"Hello?" Broc answers with a question in his voice. I'm sure he didn't recognize the phone number.

"Broc? This is Caston Black."

"Ah, fuck man. I emailed Sabrina to talk to her. Why'd she have to get you involved?"

I bang my fist on Sabrina's desk, sending a stack of paper sliding off the side. "Listen up, dipshit, Sabrina didn't get me involved. I happened to check her email because she's unavailable. Tell me what the fuck is going on."

I can hear Broc take a deep breath, possibly deciding what he wants to say to me. Then he begins saying that he's been trying to get Beth back. I wanted to laugh out loud when one of his ways to get her back was to spy and stalk her. I'm shaking when he tells me that a few weeks ago he saw Mark coming out of Beth's apartment.

"You've sat on this information for weeks? Are you insane?" I seethe.

"I've been trying to decide what to do. I knew deep down she couldn't be seeing him, but what he would be doing coming from her house has me baffled."

Getting up, I'm trying my best to not punch a hole in the wall. "Look, Broc. We're on the same side. I will make sure Beth stays safe too, but I need you to try to find out more from Mark. Can you do that for me?"

He stays silent for a long time. So long that I check to see if the phone hung up. "Broc, look, you're either with me or against me, but with me we can make sure the women we love are safe. What's it going to be?"

Taking a deep breath Broc whispers, "Fine what do you want me to do?"

Chapter Twenty-One

Sabrina

I haven't been this relaxed in months. The massage was just what I needed. I feel like a limp noodle now. We're sitting in robes, getting pedicures. Who gets to be this lucky? I'm sipping on my wine and listening to the girls chatter about who they can set Beth up with.

"Look how relaxed she is. I told you this would be perfect," Beth whispers.

"Thank you, I really am." I raise my glass. "To us, my two girls."

"To us," they respond in unison.

The rest of the flight is uneventful, and I'm even more thankful for that because I hate flying. I'm definitely feeling the effects of the wine and the lack of food from the last few hours. Even though the girls were shoving food in my face I couldn't bring myself to eat. Getting off the plane we're hit with a blast of warm humid air. I love it. Waiting for us at the bottom of the stairs of the plane is a blacked out Suburban.

I smile when I see Jake at the door. He was one of our body

154

guards in Vegas. "Jake, it's good to see you," I say when I approach him.

He's surprised when I move to hug him. "You too, Miss Bennett. It's always a pleasure."

I back up. "Jake, do we have to go over this again? Sabrina or Bre."

Sara has made it over to us. "Okay, Bre, stop attacking the guard. Sorry, Jake she's feeling no pain right now."

"Not a problem at all. I suspect it was a good flight then?" He steps aside to let us into the vehicle.

"It was!" I say it a little too loud and giggle at my enthusiasm. "Hey, Jake, are you married?"

To see a full blush cross his face makes me double over laughing.

"Okay, Sabrina, let's get you in the car." Sara guides me in through the door.

Just as she's about to get in I stick my head out of the door. "Hey, Jake."

He turns around to give me his attention.

"That's Beth over there. She needs to get—" Sara shoves my face back into the car.

"Don't mind her, but that is Beth, and she's single." With a wink and a pat on his shoulder, she gets into the car behind me.

Beth and Jake are talking outside for quite some time. When she finally gets into the car, she's flushed and full of smiles. I'm not sure if it's from the heat or what they were talking about, but I'm definitely going to find out. I don't want this weekend to be all about me.

"So, what do you think?" I nudge her knee.

Her face goes bright red. It's him. "His accent is amazing. Made me tingly all over. What is it?" Beth is on the verge of doing the 'oh my god' girl squeal.

Sara is looking at the iPod for something to listen to when she turns around with a funny look. "I don't know. It never crossed my mind to ask before," she says completely serious.

We both look over at her and bust out laughing.

Just to embarrass Beth a little more, when Jake gets in the driver seat I lean over and blurt out, "So, Beth says you make her tingly. What's that accent there, buddy? Guess I never noticed until she pointed it out." I look back over my shoulder. "I've been a little in my own world lately."

Beth wants to crawl under a rock, and Sara's trying not to laugh, but failing miserably.

Jake laughs as he blushes. "I'm from Australia."

"Oh Australian. Hear that Beth? I wonder how long he can stay down under. No, no wait, bet he can cook your shrimp on his Barbie." I try to mimic his accent and fail terribly.

All three of us fall into a hysterical laughing fit. Jake's even laughing. Sara grabs the remote for the music and starts a song that has us dancing in our seats. I've heard this song before, but never let it take a hold of me. Now I'm letting loose and going with the flow. "Party Rock" by LMFAO is blaring. Poor Jake is dealing with all of us moving around like crazy. I can't even imagine what it looks like from the outside.

We finally pull up in front of the 'Mexican Mansion'. I know Caston is extremely wealthy, but this, this is just unbelievable. We pull up along a winding cobblestone drive. Suddenly a large white house with a traditional grass roof appears. Multiple stories with balconies coming off each room. The balconies have deep brown, glossy wood rails. Every window and door in the house is open to let the perfect weather fill into the house. When the car stops Jake gets to the door quickly to let us out. I get out and feel as if I'm transported back in time to the night I pulled up in front of Caston's house.

My mouth just hangs open as I try to take in the monstrosity in front of me. Sara and Beth file out behind me, laughing.

"Holy shit, Bre." Beth stops next to me speechless, like I am.

Sara flies by us up a set of wooden steps. Beth and I do a spin in place, looking at our surroundings. I hear the Caribbean Sea, and I want nothing more than to sink my feet in the warm aqua blue water.

Sara appears in the doorway. "You slow pokes still out here? Come on!"

She turns back into the house, and I start walking up the steps. Beth stays behind. She's taking advantage of the time alone to talk with Jake and that makes me happy. Once inside, I'm taken aback again with how comfortable it is in here. I wasn't quite sure what to expect when I entered, but everything is exactly like Caston's house, very inviting and so him. I can almost picture him sitting on the couch, reading with the sun shining in filling the space with a comfortable calm.

"So, let's get into our suits and go out to the beach before the party tonight," Sara says.

"Party?" I question, skeptically.

"Don't worry, Bre. Everything will be fine."

I shake my head. Sara and her parties. I should have known. "So, where's my room?"

"Master bedroom is down this hall. You have a private wing all to yourself. I figured you would want Caston's room."

I smile and nod.

Sara turns to Beth. "And your room is—"

"I'll show her to a room." Jake interrupts.

Beth immediately stills when she hears him talk behind her. She looks at me and mouths, "Oh my God."

"Very well," Sara responds. "Meet back here in half an hour?"

"Sounds good to me," I agree.

Beth looks over to Jake, then back at us. "I'll try."

Jake offers Beth his arm, and she takes it before he leads her off in the opposite direction.

Sara and I giggle as we watch them go.

"Sara, not too crazy tonight, right?"

She crosses her heart and says, "I swear."

I just roll my eyes and head toward my room. Sara and parties are notorious for getting out of control. I'm instantly worried, but shake it off, hoping that for once she takes it easy.

After an afternoon in the sun and sand, all I want to do is head to my room and pass out. Unfortunately, Sara says it's now time to party not to nap. After we eat a quick bite, I get ready in my room. I don my short black dress that wraps to one side, making my waist look smaller than it is. I scrunched my hair with product after my shower, so the natural curls are falling around my face. I pull them up off my neck and twist them into a messy bun on the top of my head before clasping my necklace from Caston around my neck. I'm not comfortable being at a party without him, but I know he said with this around my neck no one would mess with me. I hope that's true.

Sliding on my black heels, I sit on the edge of the bed and tie up the leopard print ankle strap. I think about Caston for a moment, wondering what he's doing. I sigh deeply as I hear a light knock on my door.

"Come in."

Beth peaks her head in. She looks radiant. Her short pink dress is set off on the sun-kissed skin from this afternoon. Her hair is loose and looks perfect. She has black and white zebra stripped shoes with pink heels completing her outfit.

"Bre, are you ready? But before you head out here, I'm just warning you. There a lot of people here. I think Sara has invited the whole damn country."

I shake my head and laugh. "Of course she did. As long as you and I stay together we'll be fine."

She reaches her hand out to me, and I grab it. Jake is outside the door.

"Hey, Jake."

"Sabrina, I'm not to leave your side tonight. Orders, ma'am."

Laughing I shake my head. "I won't argue with you, Jake."

He looks relieved that I'm not going to argue with him. Beth links arms with me, and we start down the hall. I look over to her and see her hand entwined with Jake's. When we get toward the end of the hall the music is vibrating through me. The house has been cleared of all the furniture in a matter of a few hours and a dance floor and party lights have replaced them. I spot Sara with a few guys dancing suggestively to the music.

"Jake, where is our spot to 'get away', for lack of better words."

He points to an area toward the back of the house close to where the DJ is set up. Sara has spotted us now and waves us out to her. Before we have a chance to make our way out there, she comes to us.

"Come on, bitches. Let's get this party started."

Beth, Sara, and I all dance to the thumping bass of "Boom Boom Pow" by Black Eyed Peas. I'm feeling free and alone with the girls, even though we are in a room full of people. We're so full of smiles and laughs. Sweat forms on our bodies as we let the beat flow through us. I can see Jake from our spot, watching us like a hawk. I also notice the glances that go between Beth and Jake when they think no one is looking. I love that he's interested in Beth.

When the song ends, I lean over to them. "Let's sit for a bit. I need a drink." They nod their agreement.

Jake hands us each a bottle of water when we reach him. Sara takes a swig and sets it down. "Enough with the water, let's get drunk."

As if on cue "Shots" by LMFAO comes on. I just laugh. "Did you plan that?"

She holds up her hand in the Boy Scout salute. "I swear to God I didn't, but apparently God wants us to have shots."

"Let's go!" Beth says, passing out the glasses. Sara reaches behind and grabs a bottle of Tequila.

Slamming it back, we all make a face, but Sara is immediately pouring again. It doesn't take me long to feel like I'm floating. I'm a lightweight.

I start dancing again in our safe area and Sara joins me. Beth snuggles up to Jake on the couch. Sara grabs my hips moving them to the music. We sing the song at the top of our lungs. I place my hands around her neck loosely. There are butterflies in my stomach, remembering the first time we danced together. I know I need to stop myself before I lose control. Last time Caston spun me around right before anything happened.

"Stop thinking," Sara whispers in my ear and a shiver runs down my spine.

I let my head fall back and close my eyes as we continue dancing. "Dance Again" by Pitbull is on. Sara pulls me a little closer and runs her hands down my back, her hands cup my ass. Her lips graze my neck, and her tongue licks up some of the sweat on my collarbone along my necklace. I slide my hands into her hair and pull her up to my mouth. As our lips meet, I get lost in her kiss. Remembering when we were together before, my insides clench. Just as I'm about to lose control and pull her to my room to continue this in private, Caston's face flashes in my mind. I pull back, almost tumbling back onto my ass. What am I doing?

Leaving Beth, Jake's at my side in a nanosecond. He's helping me regain my footing. "I need to go to my room, Jake, I can't be out here anymore. Please, take me there."

He holds me by my elbow and guides me down the hall. Hearing Sara rush after us, I plead with Jake, "Please don't let anyone in. I—I just can't face her right now."

Once I'm in my room, I shut the door and hear Jake stop Sara before she can enter. "Sorry, Sara, she wants to be alone. Why don't you go back to the party?"

I can hear her heels on the tile heading away from the door. I crack it open and Jake looks in at me. "She's gone."

"Thank you, Jake. Please, go back to the party and have fun with Beth. I'll lock the door."

"If you would, please allow me to check the room before I leave?"

I open the door and let him pass before, glancing to the end of the hall. I catch Sara watching me. We hold each other's gaze for a moment before I drop it and shut the door behind Jake.

He quickly scans the room before heading toward the door to let himself out. Before he goes I stop him. "Jake?"

"Yes, can I get you something?"

"My phone. I need to talk to Caston."

"Of course, Sabrina. I'll be back in a minute."

He shuts the door behind him, and I sink to the floor at the end of the bed, tears start streaming down my face. How could I let myself get out of control like that? How is Caston going to react?

I undo my shoes and let them fall to the side of me. Jake's back quickly like he promised. He also has brought with him a bottle of water and aspirin. He doesn't say anything about my tears, which I'm thankful for. Once he leaves, I lock the door and strip down. Letting my hair fall down my back, I climb into bed and lay on the side of the bed that Caston usually sleeps on hugging his pillow tight. Before I have a chance to call him I fall asleep.

Chapter Twenty-Two

Caston

Terrance has finally enlightened me to all of the security details that he's been keeping from me. To say I'm furious is an understatement. When I told him about Broc's email and Mark, he didn't seem surprised. Once we were at the airport waiting for my plane to return, he filled me in.

"Sir, I apologize I haven't been forthcoming." Terrance stands by the doorway in the waiting room.

"Terrance, if you want to keep your job with me, never, ever, keep anything from me again."

He nods and pulls out his phone to confirm the plane should be ready for take-off in a half hour. I motion for him to sit because I need to know everything.

"Please, tell me everything again, so I know what I've been missing all these months."

Once he is seated, he clears his throat. "Since Sabrina's shooting I've had extra security added undercover throughout all of your companies. They're working as regular employees and have been filling me in on anything out of the ordinary."

"Who are they?"

"Sir," Terrance looks a little uneasy, "I'd rather not say."

I nod. I'm not happy about it, but I can understand it.

"Well, after the shooting I started tracking Beverly's off shore accounts and noticed that there was a regular amount being taken out. I knew it wasn't for James because his accounts never went up in those increments. I got Will on it, and he did some digging. That's when we found out Mark was involved with her."

"You knew this whole time and never told me?" I seethe through my teeth.

"Sir, it was for everyone's safety. Please, understand that. We've been tracking his activities and following him, so I know what he's been up too. He's followed the girls a few times."

"WHAT!" I jump out of my seat and have Terrance by the neck of his shirt.

Somehow Terrance stays calm with me in his face. "We've had people following him, so he would have never gotten close."

Loosening my grip, I sit back down and run my hands through my hair. "How did I not see this?"

"Sir, that's my job. You were focused on Sabrina getting better, as you should be."

"Who's been following Mark?"

"Well, it was Jake." Knowing that Jake was assigned to watch over the girls this weekend, my head snaps up. Terrance holds his hand out for me to calm down. "I've also had someone get close with Mark. We have an inside advantage now."

"What? Terrance, what are you saying?"

Before Terrance has a chance to answer the question my cell chimes. I check the message; it's the notification that the plane is ready for us. Once we get to the plane, I don't continue my conversation with Terrance. I know he has things worked out. The bottom line is I trust him, I just wish he would have told me instead of me finding out from Broc.

I'm anxious the entire flight to Mexico. I'm worried about what Mark could be planning, and I need to get to Sabrina. What's even worse is I've been trying to reach Jake, but his phone keeps going to voicemail, and no one is answering at the house. My heart is in my throat by the time we land. Terrance knows of my reluctance to let Sabrina go to Mexico to begin with, but Sara talked me into it, just like she usually can. Damn her!

Descending the stairs the heat hits me like a slap in the face. It's dark, but the runway is lit up like Christmas. I make my way across the tarmac to the waiting car. Terrance opens the car door, gets in the driver's seat, and begins the thirty minute drive to the villa.

The tension in the car is so thick you could cut it with a knife. What will we find when we get there? Would she be okay? My heart's beating a million miles a minute. I close my eyes and lift my head up, sending up a silent prayer that everyone is safe.

I see the lights of the villa in the distance and my stomach turns over. There are some vans in the driveway. I shake my head, knowing exactly who they are. Sara had gone and thrown a party, even though she promised she wouldn't.

"Terrance, what the fuck? How did she do this?"

He shakes his head. "You know Sara."

I let out an exasperated sigh.

When Terrance stops the car, I get out before he can open my door. The cleanup crew greets me as they're carrying the furniture back into the house.

"When did the party end?" I ask one of them.

"It was still supposed to be going on, but there was some sort of incident and everyone left. We decided to just clean early. I hope that is okay, sir?"

I clasp him on the shoulder. "Of course."

Terrance walks up, so I fill him in on the situation. "There was some sort of incident that ended the party early."

Making my way through the open door, everything is silent. Terrance takes his phone out of his pocket and dials Jake again. Through the silence we hear the ringing. Walking in the direction of the sound, we find it wedged in a crease of a chair.

"Fuck! That explains why he wasn't answering us. When I find him, he's fucking done," Terrance declares.

I'm pulled toward the wing of the house that has the master bedroom in it. I feel the electricity flow through me when I reach the room. Stopping in front of the door, I reach down to the knob. I know she is on the other side. I test the door and it's locked.

"I'm going to go to the balcony and go in that way. I can't imagine she is in trouble. There would be a lot more going on around here if there was."

Terrance nods and waits by the door as I make my way to the balcony.

Once inside the room, the fan on the ceiling makes a humming noise, but the sound of the waves crashing on the beach almost drowns it out. Looking toward the bed, I find her illuminated by the moonlight. She looks like an angel sleeping safe and sound. I turn to Terrance and just nod. He returns the nod and walks back down the hall, leaving me with my girl.

Finally able to let the breath I've been holding this whole trip out, I walk to the chair by the window and begin to undress. My eyes never leave her, though. Her rhythmic breathing, the white sheet draped over her sun-kissed skin rising slightly with each breath. Her hair is fanned out on the pillow behind her. She's curled up clutching a pillow on my side of the bed.

Slowly moving toward the bed, I see her phone light up on the floor. Grabbing it I turn it over. All of my phone calls and voicemails are there. Then I see all the texts from Sara. The last one was from her.

I'm so sorry.

What the fuck happened? I turn the phone off and set it on the table next to the bed. Slowly moving the sheet, I slide in behind her and pull her into my embrace.

"Caston?" she mummers sleepily, her voice barely audible.

"Sleep, baby." I kiss her shoulder and pull her closer.

Her breathing returns to a steady rhythm, and I know she has fallen asleep once again.

The morning light brightens the room, and I feel her stir in my arms. Our legs are tangled among the sheets like usual. The relaxing sound of waves crashing makes me want to stay in here all day with her in my arms.

Feeling her stir again, I crack my eyes and see hers flutter open.

"Are you really here, or am I dreaming?" she whispers, trying not to break the spell if she's dreaming.

"I'm here, sweetheart." I place a kiss on her nose.

I know she's still not awake because she nuzzles her head under my chin, and I feel her relax again in my arms.

It's been another hour or so before she starts to stir again. This time I tip her head up and place a deep kiss on her lips, letting our tongues mingle and dance over each other. Once I withdraw, she rolls to her back and rests a hand over her head.

"Caston, you know I love waking up to you."

I can sense a but coming. I let my finger tip trace the side of her body before circling her plump breast and then her peaked nipple.

"But," I urge her to go on.

"Why are you here?" Her eyes open and lock with mine.

Her breath hitches when I pinch the nipple hard.

"You're so beautiful."

She runs the hand that was above her head through her hair and sits up, allowing the sheet fall to her waist.

"Nope, not going to distract me."

I roll to my back and laugh. She knows me too well.

"Okay, but can I have another kiss first?"

She licks her lips as she moves toward me. Stopping millimeters from my lips she demands, "Answer me."

I reach up, sliding my hands in her hair and pull her toward me, our lips colliding together. She taste like heaven. I can't get enough of her. She doesn't break our kiss, but she lifts up and straddles my lap.

I can feel her moisture through the fabric of my boxers and her panties. I know she's missed me too, but I need to tell her what brought me to her last night.

She sits back, and I enjoy the view of her bare breasts on display for me. I sit up and wrap my arms around her waist as I scoot back to rest my back on the headboard.

I know she can see the worry in my eyes because she tenses up. I stroke her cheek. "I hate to see you frown."

"I know something is wrong. You wouldn't be here if everything was okay."

I flash my wicked smirk. "Are you sure about that? You know I can't get enough of you."

The blush I love so much creeps up her cheeks, giving them a rosy glow.

I let my arms slide down to rest on her thighs. "After you called, I continued working, all but forgetting to check your email like you asked me to."

She giggles. "You didn't have to come all this way to tell me that."

"Bre," I raise my eyebrow to her, "I'm not that desperate. May I continue?"

She nods her head with a smirk of her own.

"So anyways," I try to sound annoyed, but fail miserably, "when I did get to your office and checked your email, you had three emails from Broc."

I can see her confusion on her face. "Why the fuck would he be emailing me?"

"Exactly what I thought. So I opened them. Sorry."

"Don't be," she says as she's tracing the lines of my abdominal muscles, making me lose my train of thought.

"Bre, you're not making it easy for me to concentrate."

Her smile is evil, and she wiggles her hips in my lap.

I laugh and shake my head. "So, as I was saying, I opened them. Well, to sum it up he was concerned for your safety."

She shakes her head. "That doesn't make sense. Why would he be concerned for my safety? What aren't you telling me, Caston?"

I can see the worry on her face again. "He said that he has been lurking around Beth's apartment, trying to get her to agree to meet with him. He said he saw Mark coming out of Beth's apartment a few weeks ago."

"Now, Caston that's just silly. Why would he have—"

"He said he drives by Beth's occasionally to check on her place, and he saw Mark walking out of her place."

Anger flashes over her face. Not what I was expecting. She scrambles off my lap before I can explain what I learned from Terrance. I try to grab for her, but she gets tangled in sheets, and we both go tumbling to the ground. Getting away from me again, she grabs her long t-shirt and flings the door open.

Chapter Twenty-Three

Sabrina

I scramble off of Caston's lap so fast we fall to the floor. How the fuck could she do this to me? I thought we were friends. I haven't moved this fast in a long time.

"Bre! Sabrina, stop." Caston is stumbling to get his pants on as he chases after me down the hall.

Thoughts are flying around my head. I make it into the main room and see Sara at the breakfast bar. I pause for a minute as our eyes meet. Caston comes to a sudden halt behind me, almost knocking me over.

"Bre, let's calm down."

I turn my head to look at him. "No, Caston. I want answers now."

"Sabrina." Sara's voice quivers hesitantly on my name.

Looking back over at her, my eyes narrow. "Not now," I hiss as I turn on my heels and head toward the stairs to confront Beth.

I hear Caston behind me say to Sara, "What the fuck happened?"

Not waiting to hear her answer, I grip the banister and head up the stairs. My mind is once again swirling with all sorts of scenarios.

"Beth!" I scream when I get to the top of the steps.

I make my way to the door of the room she's staying in. Caston just hit the top of the stairs, and I know he'll stop me if I don't do this now.

Flinging her door open, there's a scrambling of body limbs trying to cover up with the sheet. I walk further into the room.

"Beth! Look at me. I need you to fucking look at me." My voice raises and cracks as I continue to make my way to the bed.

Caston walks up behind me, placing a hand on mine. "Bre, not now. Let's calm down."

Just then a head pop up from the covers. My mouth falls open. "Jake."

Just as I was about to apologize for walking into the wrong room Beth's head slowly makes its way to the surface.

I'm momentarily speechless as I stare at the two of them in bed together.

Caston pulls me back toward him. "Let's leave them alone," he whispers in my ear. His words bring back why I'm here.

"No." I twist out of his hold. "No, Caston. I'm tired of people fucking with me."

Beth sits up straighter. Thankfully holding on to the sheet. "Bre, what's wrong?"

"No. You don't get to ask me questions. I'm asking the questions." I point to myself to try to make my point.

"Okay," she says quietly, trying to look past me at Caston.

"Why are you fucking around with Mark?" I yell at her.

"What?" she says in stunned disbelief, like she heard me wrong.

"You fucking heard me, Beth. What are you doing fucking around with Mark? After all we've been through, what I've been through?"

"I don't know what you're talking about." Her brow is crinkled in confusion.

"Cut the crap, Beth. Broc emailed me and told me he saw Mark coming out of your apartment. Explain that to me, Beth. Explain why Mark was coming out of your fucking apartment if you're not fucking around with him."

Her head is shaking violently, and I see tears welling up in her eyes. "Bre, you have to believe me."

I get closer to her. "How could you?"

"I never, I could never." The tears started to fall and her voice was a whisper.

"Beth, Broc said he saw him."

I see Jake move a little and reach for something on the side of the bed. He comes back up with a white shirt and hands it over to Beth.

"Thank you," she says through her tears. He tenderly strokes her hair before placing a hand on her back.

"Bre, you have to believe me. I would never have anything to do with that asshole. Ever! He should be behind bars. Right now I'm not sure what I'm more worried about the fact that Broc was stalking me, the fact that Mark was coming out of my apartment, or the fact that you don't fucking believe me?"

She scrambles out of the bed, dragging me into the attached bathroom for privacy. Her hands grasp my forearms. "Bre, you have to believe me."

We're both in tears now. She shakes me a little. "Tell me you believe me. Damn, Bre, I've been through so much with you because of Mark. Do you really think I'd be with him?"

Pulling her into a hug, I sob into her shoulder. "Beth, what does he want? Why can't I just be rid of him? If you aren't seeing him, why was he coming out of your house?"

We pull apart, and Beth looks at me with worry in her eyes. "I don't know."

When we come out of the bathroom Caston and Jake are talking quietly. They look like they are arguing, but once we appear, they part. Caston walks out of the room looking upset.

"Beth, I need to make a few calls. Will you be okay for a minute?" Jake asks Beth.

She bites her lip. "Yes," she whispers.

I move out of Beth's hold and sit on the edge of her bed. She sits next to me, and we both watch him walk out of the room. Grabbing her hand, I squeeze it.

"I'm sorry, Beth. I don't know what came over me. I felt so betrayed and the way my life has been taking twists and turns, I didn't know what to believe."

She puts her arm around my shoulder and pulls my head down to rest on her shoulder. "It's okay, Bre. I understand, but you have to believe me. I'd rather die than to get involved with him."

We sit for a few minutes in silence. "Bre, I'm scared. Why was he in my apartment?"

I sit up and look at her. "I don't know, but Caston and Jake will find out."

She nods, and our attention is drawn to the doorway. Jake has reappeared. I feel Beth shudder at the sight of him.

"I'll leave you two alone. Beth, I can't apologize enough, I'm so sorry."

I leave her side and make my way to the doorway. I stop a few inches from Jake. "You screw her over and I'll kill you."

"I'd never." He responds to me, but never takes his eyes off of her.

I walk past him to find Caston leaning on the wall, his foot propped up, and his arms crossed over his bare chest. He looks so god damn sexy standing there in his shorts. His messy, just fucked hair and sparkling blue eyes make me lick my lips. I want him.

"Bre, you could have waited until I told you everything. I knew Beth wasn't involved with him." His tone is almost a warning.

Rushing up into his arms, I press my body to his. "I'm sorry. I feel like a fool." He accepts me into his embrace, and my heart skips a beat.

I look up to meet his eyes. A deep rumble sounds in his throat as I'm swept up into his arms and cradled to his chest. I snuggle into him as he descends the stairs and heads back to our room.

Sliding my hands through his hair, I grip it and tug. Once we make it back into our room, he slams the door shut with his foot. Walking over to the bed, he throws me down with a wicked smirk on his face. His hands undo his shorts, and as he shoves them down, his cock springs out. I suck in a breath at the sight of him. I'm not sure I will ever tire of looking at this magnificent man in front of me.

Feeling overdressed, I pull my shirt over my head, leaving only my panties. "Fuck, you're so perfect," Caston growls.

I clench my legs to try to relieve the ache. Grabbing my feet Caston slides me down to the edge of the bed and kneels in front of me.

"I can smell you, Bre. You're wet for me already, aren't you?"

My hands are on my breasts, kneading them and tugging at my nipples. His head lowers between my thighs, and he bites my pussy through the cotton fabric. My head flies back to the mattress. His mouth isn't even on my skin, and I'm already about to come.

"Fuck, Caston." My hands grasp his hair again.

His strong hands make their way up my legs, and his fingers hook my panties. He swiftly pulls them down without even missing a beat on my pussy. Feeling his mouth pressed to my hot flesh sends me spiraling into bliss.

His mouth leaves my wet lips and makes his way up my body, trailing light kisses along the way.

"Caston." It's a breathless plea, for what I'm not exactly sure, but I know he will take care of me.

He comes to my nipple, and his tongue darts out and traces a circle around my peak. When his teeth nip at it, I let out a small cry.

Just when I feel as though I can't take anymore, he slides into me. Just an inch to begin. He knows it will drive me crazy with want.

"Do you want me, Bre?" His eyes look down on me with a heat that makes me feel so alive.

"You know I do."

"Tell me."

"Caston, please. I need you. I need you inside of me. I want to feel you fuck me hard. Fuck me like it might be the last time."

Just as I finish speaking, he shoves himself into me completely. His body meets mine, and I scream out his name as he pounds into me harder than he ever has before. It's exactly what I needed. We are one. It feels special. Different. I can't place what the difference is, but we're one. There's no telling where he ends and I begin. I'm about to lose myself again.

"Fuck, Bre. You're so fucking hot. So wet for me."

"I'm coming, Caston." My body shudders, and I lose myself to him. I pull him down to me, needing him close. As my lips crash to his, I feel him find his own release deep inside me. My belly flutters accepting all he has to give. I can't get enough.

We lay in each other's arms for a while, not wanting to lose contact. My fingers slide up and down his spine mindlessly. Right now it's just us.

"Caston?"

I hate breaking this peaceful moment, but I need to know.

"Yes, baby."

"Is everything going to be okay?"

His shoulders flex and he tenses. Lifting his head to look into my eyes he says, "I'm not sure." Letting his finger trace down my cheek he continues, "I'm not sure, and that scares the fucking shit out of me."

Chapter Twenty-Four

Mark

Kaitlyn's time in town is up, and I'm actually sad to see her go. She was a good lay that gave me a run for my money, dare I say I was falling harder for her than I thought possible. I was able to keep my side job a secret from her, and I hope once I'm done with it we might be together again.

It's been a week since I've seen any action worth mentioning with Caston or Sabrina. I know the wedding is coming up, so it's been ridiculous flower, cake, dress fitting meetings. Shoot me in the head. I'm never getting married.

I open my phone and see a text from Broc. Weird, it's been months. Just as I'm about to open it my phone lights up. I see that it's a restricted call.

"Hello?"

"Mark. I'm being released in a few hours."

I'm already on my feet, reaching for my keys. "I'm on my way."

"Mark?"

"Yes, ma'am."

"That bitch whore better not be there."

I'm momentarily caught off guard. Composing myself, I whisper, "No, ma'am, she's not."

The phone hangs up and a cool shiver goes through my body. Is it excitement that I get to be with Mistress again, or is it something else?

I reach the jail in plenty of time, so I wait in the car for a little while. Remembering the text, I pull out my phone and read it.

Hoping to put our past behind us. Number is still the same. -Broc

Odd. Why now?

I don't really have time to think about it before I see my Mistress strolling toward my Charger. Even after being in jail, she's looking better than ever.

Getting out, I walk to her side of the car. I smirk as I look up and down her legs. Opening the door when she's close, I acknowledge her. "Mistress."

She smiles wickedly and leans in to kiss my cheek. "Mark."

Kiss and a nip. She slides gracefully into the car.

When I get behind the wheel, she immediately starts questioning me. "What news do you have for me? Now that I'm out, for good, I want to get this finished. I knew they'd have nothing to stand on once they found out that the bullet in Sabrina didn't come from my gun."

She smiles wickedly over at me. I remember when we came up with the plan to have me shoot her instead of Beverly. It was genius really. They would do surgery, analyze the bullet. Beverly was going to plead not guilty, saying she was only holding her gun up out of self-defense. Getting charged at by Sabrina, Terrance, and Caston scared her. Thinking of her being scared makes me laugh.

"They still have me on that fucked up restraining order. You'll have to continue on as planned, since I can't go near them without sending the red flags up."

I nod.

Her evil smile lighting up her face in a way that used to thrill me, but I now find slightly—*disturbing?* "Our judicial system is so fucked up."

My mind drifts off. I know that all too well. That's how that asshole got free before he killed my mom.

Sitting in history class I feel my cellphone go off. Brother Ed has been going on about the Civil War for almost an hour. Waiting for him to turn around I reach into my pocket just as it goes off again. It's my home number.

Fuck! Glancing at the clock I see there is only two minutes of class left. Surely it can wait two minutes. Those were the longest minutes of my life. Time seemed to stand still. I've never moved as fast as I did when the bell went off.

Pushing my way through the hall, I tried to make it seem like I was being a jerk and not scared out of my mind for my mom. Clasping hands with some friends on the way to the restroom and a few kisses on the cheerleaders' cheeks makes everything seem A-Okay.

I finally make it to the restroom and lock the door. After checking to make sure it's empty, I dial my home number. I tap my foot quickly and slide my finger under my collar of my polo. Fucking uniforms are so stiff. Three rings and no answer. Five. Ten. Then the phone connects, but there's nothing but the sound of air.

I clutch the phone, calling out, "Mom?"

Nothing. No sound.

"Mom, are you okay?"

Silence.

"Mom? Please, say something."

This time I hear a deep wheezing breath. Now I'm scared. That sound isn't normal.

"Did he hurt you? If he hurt you... Mom, if he hurt you press a button."

There is a pause, a wheeze, and then BEEP.

Fuck! "Mom, I'll be right there. You hear me. I'm coming."

I don't even hang up the phone. Bursting through the doors of the restroom I run in a full sprint to the car. I can hear the principal running after me, but I know she won't be able to catch up. Plus, I don't care if I have to run her over. I have to get to my mom.

I snap back to reality. Looking over at Beverly to see if she noticed my distraction. She didn't, thankfully. She was too busy looking at herself in mirror.

"See something you like, big boy?"

For the first time, since I met her, I'm not ready to fall to my knees for her. Thankfully, we pull up to the condo before I have to answer. She waits for me to open her door, but she takes off into the condo before I can even shut the door.

There's a tense silence between us.

"I need a hot bath. This jail grime needs to be soaked off for hours."

"Can I bring you some wine?"

She stops on her way to the bedroom, looking over her shoulder. "What do you think?"

I cringe, stupid me.

In the kitchen, I reach up to grab a wine glass and a bottle of merlot. I'm so used to having my music blaring when I'm home the silence is nerve wrecking. So much so that I almost drop the glass and wine bottle when my phone goes off.

Damn, Mark, hold your shit together, I scold myself.

Quickly shifting the items to my other hand, I reach into my pocket. Kaitlyn's picture lights up the screen.

"Hey, baby," I answer.

"Hey. I miss you."

Moving to the patio, so I wouldn't be heard, I lean up on the fence. "You have no idea. I want to see you."

"I have two more weeks of non-stop travels for work. Then I was originally planning on heading home, but I could come to see you?" Her voice breaks at the end as if she is unsure if she overstepped.

I run my free hand through my hair. Am I really going to ask to see her again? I can't believe I'm even considering this. What are these feelings? Relationships with feelings aren't really my thing, but something is different with Kaitlyn.

"Oh baby, I'd love to have you stay with me, or I can go with you."

Okay, no turning back now. The sentiment has been spoken out loud.

"Really?" She squeaks.

A smile creeps over my face. "Really."

I can hear the smile spread over her face just by the way she's talking.

"Kaitlyn, I have to go. I'll call you back tonight. Will that be okay?"

"Of course. Bye, Mark."

Hanging up, I quickly head back inside and toward the bathroom to give the wine to Beverly.

The room is full of steam. I can see her resting her head back on a bath pillow. Bubbles threaten to spill over the top of the tub. Jasmine wafts through the air.

"About time you brought my wine." She doesn't even open her eyes when she holds out her hand for me to place the glass in.

"Once I finish this job for you, I'm done."

I place the glass in her hand and turn to leave the room as I hear her shift, making water slosh over the side. I can only assume she's sitting up, but I don't look behind me to find out. I won't give her an inkling that I'm afraid of her. She would feed off of it and hold it against me.

This is *my* place, I'm not going to walk on eggshells around her. Walking into the living room, I pick up the remote and turn on "Radioactive" by Imagine Dragons, turning it up loud. A lot louder than I normally would, but I want to make a point.

This is it. Exactly as the song says. Welcome to the new age. My age; my time.

I sit on the brown leather couch and cross my leg, resting my ankle on my opposite knee. Staring at the doorway between the rooms. A foreboding sense of doom fills me, but I won't give up.

No more will anyone run me. It started with Ric, my step-dad, moved to my coaches, and now it's her. I want to run my life. My soul is alive for the first time.

As the music pumps through me, she suddenly appears.

"Turn this shit down." Her face is hard and unrelenting.

My eyes harden. I shake my head slowly, purposely. I've woken up.

She walks over to me and smacks me across the face. I don't even flinch. I can tell she is flustered when I don't give in to her. She backs up a few steps, almost stumbling over the coffee table.

"What the fuck is wrong with you? You respect me."

I stare at her. I don't speak. I hold my ground.

"Mark, kneel. NOW."

I want to fuck with her, so I stand up. Towering over her, I look down and see her straighten her spine. An evil smile crosses her face, but I intend to wipe it right back off.

"Kneel," she commands, but I hear that slight crack in her voice.

She's now mine. I control her. Placing my hands on her shoulders I press down. She resists at first, but she finally gives up and sinks to her knees. I'm stronger than she is physically, and now I have the motivation to take back the control of my life.

Welcome to the new age.

I'm the master now.

Chapter Twenty-Five

Caston

We're on high alert since Broc's email. Terrance and I scheduled a meeting with him back at my office in a few days to see what he knows. Right now we're relaxing in Mexico, and Sabrina is safe in my arms.

We lie on the outdoor bed on our balcony. The sun makes her hair shine with an auburn highlights. The slight wave is more prominent because of the humidity. I listen to the waves crash onto the shore. It's so peaceful.

Her finger slowly traces a swirl pattern around my muscles, sending a shiver to run through me in this heat.

"I love listening to your heart," she says it so quietly I almost didn't hear her.

Turning my head, I place a kiss on the top of her head. I take a deep breath, but don't say anything. I don't want to distract her thoughts. She's been tense since I arrived. Isolating herself, avoiding Sara, staying quiet—she's making me very worried.

"Your heart and the waves crashing make the perfect

combination." She shifts so she's resting her chin on my chest, staring up at my eyes.

I place one arm around her and stroke her back with my thumb while the other hand goes behind my head. "What's going on, Bre? What has you so worried?"

She bites on her bottom lip, and her eyes leave mine.

"Nope, I'm not going to let you get away with that today." I shift, so I'm sitting up a little more and cup her cheek to make her look back at me.

Tears are threatening to fall from her eyes. "I'm scared, Caston."

I pull her up into my arms and cradle her. "What is there to be afraid of?"

"This crazy path my life has led me on. I'm scared that I'm going to wake up, and it's all been a dream. We've been through so much and made it through. One day we aren't going to be so lucky, then what am I going to do?"

"Baby, I can assure you this isn't a dream. You and I, we're in it for the long haul. Nothing can take you away from me. We've made it this far. I promise you, we'll make it through anything. Honey, look at me." Her glistening eyes shift and meet mine. "There's something else wrong. You've been distant."

Her eyes widen as if she was caught doing something wrong. She tries to scoot off my lap, but I pull her closer.

"You aren't going to get away that easily. Don't make me resort to tickling you." Sliding my hand up the side of her body, I already have her squirming.

"Okay, okay. I can't handle you tickling me."

My hand stops.

She takes a deep breath in, blows it out, and now she's making me nervous. "Caston, I had a moment with Sara, when you weren't here. I feel so guilty. It shouldn't have happened. I pushed her away as soon as I came to my senses. I don't know what came over me. I'm not usually so reckless, but the music and alcohol were flowing through me. Not to mention the damn dancing—"

I silence her with a kiss. She backs away from me. "Nothing happened between you the two of you."

"We kissed Caston, I wanted it to go further. That makes it so wrong."

"Bre, I've seen you kiss her before." She turns a beautiful shade of red and looks away. "You're fucking hot as hell when you kiss her."

"But, Caston, you weren't there. What if I didn't stop? That's cheating. I couldn't live with myself."

I move her, so she's looking at me again. "Bre, you didn't, you stopped. I saw you in the club when you were dancing with her, remember? If I hadn't stopped you then it would have happened that night too. Do I think it would have gone farther? I'm not sure. I would hope that Sara would respect me enough to stop if I'm not there. They have an open relationship, but I don't want that with you. Yes, we have been with them, but Sara is the only one that has done anything with you. I'd never let another man lay his hands on you. Sabrina, I trust you. I don't want this to be a source of tension between you two."

She nods and whispers, "She's intoxicating. It's confusing."

Laughing, I grab her face and pull her into a deep kiss that leaves us both breathless.

"You're intoxicating."

I'm fucking hard as granite thinking about them together, but I need to have her get all her worries out. I know there's something else on her mind because she pulls her legs up into a hug and stares out over the ocean.

I rearrange my hard on and once again pull her down into my lap. Stoking the hair that has fallen away from her eyes.

Thankfully, she spills what else is bothering her before I have to push her to say it.

"I'm scared to get married."

I stiffen, stilling my hand on her hair. My heart feels like it just plummeted into my stomach. Is she saying she doesn't want to get married?

"Okay." My voice cracks a bit.

Immediately she sits up.

"Oh God, Caston. I still want to marry you. That's not what I'm saying." She places a kiss on my lips lightly.

I feel my heart begin to beat again.

"Fuck, Sabrina, you scared the shit out of me."

I kiss her again and again.

She giggles and lets me kiss her. I feel her smile widen on my shoulder when I pull her into a hug.

"I'm sorry. That came out wrong. I'm scared to get married in front of all those people I don't know. All those eyes on me, judging me."

She takes a deep breath and blows it out. I know she's really upset because her parents won't be there.

"Those eyes who judge are just jealous of you. Don't let them get to you. Bre, you know your parents will be there, right?"

She starts crying again and nods her head. "I've felt them so much the last few months. It's like you've brought them back into my mind."

I smile. That makes me feel so amazing. I love to bring her happiness. I want to be her strength when she feels like it's gone.

I take her in my arms and pull her close again. "I promise you, I will do everything in my power to keep you feeling them."

Sliding my hands into her hair, I pull her mouth to mine. We get lost in each other's kiss.

Chapter Twenty-Six

Mark

I like, no *love*, having Beverly as my submissive. I've fuckin' given that bitch what she deserves over and over again. I stretch out in bed and grab my phone. Needing my love, not my sub, I dial up Kaitlyn.

"Mark, I was just thinking about you."

I smile when I hear her voice and that I just thought of her as my love. "When do I get to see you again?"

Hearing her laugh makes my cock jump. Taking it in my hand I wait for her to answer. "Few weeks, maybe sooner."

I let out a growl. "Fuck, I can't wait that long. My balls are going to go blue."

"You haven't?" She sounds kind of shocked.

"No, baby, something about you has my heart in knots. Since you, it's only been you."

"Mark..." She sounds like she doesn't believe me. That pisses me off.

I sit up straighter in bed. "Are you saying you've been with someone else?" I'm about to throw my phone across the room.

"No, but I don't have time to go out." Her voice is barely audible.

"Don't fuck with me, Kaitlyn. If there's been someone else, you better fucking tell me."

I can almost see her cringe over the phone, her eyes cast downward. "No, Mark, only you."

Relaxing a bit, I roll my head on my shoulders. "There better fucking not be."

I hear a girl's voice in the background, and she moves to cover the phone. "Mark, I gotta go. Work calls."

"Okay, baby."

"Bye, Mark."

"Bye, baby. Oh and, baby?"

"Yes." Her voice waivers just a bit.

"I'm sorry for snapping. I just don't want anyone else to have that sweet pussy of yours. It's mine. You got it?"

"Okay."

I can still tell she's apprehensive. "Say it, Kaitlyn."

She whispers into the phone, making it sound breathy, "My pussy is all yours."

"Good girl. Now snap me a picture of that sweet thing and send it to me. I'll see you soon, love."

I hang up and make my way to the bathroom before slipping into some black sweats. My phone chimes alerting me to a text. With the flip of a finger I see the beautiful, slick pussy I've been dreaming of. I'll make use of that picture later, but now I'm starving.

Walking to the kitchen, I find Beverly in there trying to cook and failing miserably.

I walk up behind her and take her by the shoulders. "Get out of the fucking kitchen before you burn the fucking place down."

Shoving her away forcefully, she loses her balance and falls to the floor. "Stay down there, bitch."

She does as she's told. Rolling my eyes, I move to the balcony door and open it to let the smoke out and throw away the burned shit in the pan.

"I'm meeting with Broc today. We have two weeks until the wedding. Which means two weeks until I'm done with you. So help me God, you better find someplace else to be because once it's done. I'm done."

"But, sir—"

I turn around and back hand her. "Beverly, I didn't give you permission to talk to me. Get out of my fucking sight."

Her eyes snap up to mine. I see a hint of dominance trying to break free. I pull her up by her arm and drag her to the couch. Shoving her down as I rip her shirt.

"Is this what you want? Do you want me to fuck you, Beverly?"

"Yes, please, Mark."

I palm her breasts the disgusting fake globes. I hate the feel of fake shit. She lets out a moan, and her head falls back. I smack them a few times, making them red.

"Yes, Mark. Fuck."

I know she's on the brink, just from me touching and smacking her breasts. Fuck this.

Just as quickly as I shoved her down, I turn and walk away.

"Mark, oh God, no."

"Fuck off, Beverly. You're a washed up old whore."

"You'll pay, Mark," She screams down the hall.

I laugh on my way back to my room. "Not a chance, bitch."

Walking into my room, I strip out of my pants and locate my jeans and t-shirt. Once I'm dressed, I grab my keys and head out to my car to meet Broc for an early lunch. Beverly has made herself scarce.

Good thing I have my guns locked up, or I'm sure I'd be in a world of hurt.

I arrive a few minutes early and sit in my car to scope out the place we're meeting. Something doesn't seem right, but I just can't put my finger on it. Deciding that I'm full of shit, I get out and cross the street, making my way to the diner.

Once I walk in, I look around again. Everyone seems quiet and peaceful. Keeping to themselves. No one even looked up when I walked in. Seeing the please seat yourself sign, I make my way to a corner booth that seems somewhat private. I sit so my back is to the wall. No one can come up to surprise me from behind. That much I've learned, never leave your back uncovered.

I pull my phone out to go over some notes on my plan for the next few weeks to finish this job. Before I have a chance to get lost in my thoughts, I see somebody walk up to the table.

Glancing up, Broc's smiling down at me.

"Hey, buddy," he says much too cheerfully.

I slide out of the booth and do the whole half, smack your back man hug. "Broc, long time, man."

We both take our seats and the waitress comes over instantly with two glasses of water. After quickly glancing at our menus, we place our order.

"She's got a nice ass, doesn't she?" Broc says.

I shrug my shoulders. Kaitlyn's is much more divine. He's wringing his hands on the table. He was never good at lying or playing cool.

"What's up there, *buddy*?" I say condescendingly, nudging my chin toward his hands that are now making me nervous. I glance around the diner again to take in my surroundings.

"Me, oh nothing, nothing. Just wanted to catch up. I'm back in town. Just thought…"

Is there a bead of sweat forming on his brow? I laugh lightly, sit back, and place my arms on the back of the booth back. I play cool as a cucumber, but really my senses are on high alert.

"Bull shit." His mouth falls open. "Spill it. Why'd you contact me? Does it have to do with Beth?"

His hands ball into fists.

"Ding, ding, ding. We have a winner folks," I proclaim sarcastically.

If this was a cartoon, I would probably be able to see steam coming out of Broc's ears and his face turn an unnatural shade of red. The visual thought of it makes me laugh.

He pounds the table, making the silverware clink. His little temper tantrum also turns a few heads.

"Oh, now who has the temper?"

"Don't you fucking, dare," Broc says through gritted teeth, his finger pointing at me.

I lean forward on the table, resting on my arms. "Don't I dare what exactly?"

"I saw you." He rubs the back of his hand over his mouth. "I saw you coming out of her apartment. Stay the fuck away from her."

"Ha! You think I'd want a piece of her used pussy?"

That pushes his buttons further. "Fuck you, Mark."

"You're not really my type, Broc"

He reaches across the table and grabs my black t-shirt by the neck. "I've fucking contacted Caston Black. He's on to you, you sick fuck. Stay away from Beth, or you'll pay."

Shoving him back into his seat, I straighten my shirt. "You're fucking insane, Broc." Still keeping my cool. "I don't know what crack you are smokin', but you need to lay off. I'm not fucking with Beth, and I sure as hell haven't seen or associated with Sabrina for months. I've got a redheaded beauty to call my own now."

"You can't be trusted, Mark." He's seething.

All I can do is laugh. A laugh I know sounds evil. "And you can? I remember you standing behind me for a very long time, not doing anything to help Bre when I was wailing on her."

His eyes grow wide. Got him there. He didn't do a god damn thing to help her or stop me, even though he knew what I was doing.

The waitress brings our food and quickly leaves us again.

"I'm not even fucking hungry." He shoves the plate toward the middle of the table. Moving out of the booth, he throws down some money to cover his part of the bill and points at me. "Just stay the fuck away from Beth."

I hold my hands up in surrender, even though I'm doing no such thing. He turns to leave, and I just shake my head before diving into my plate of overflowing food. I'm so fucking hungry.

Concentrating on devouring my food, I don't look up immediately when someone comes up to the table and stands before me. I can tell by the pants it's a man, so it isn't worth my time. I'm annoyed that whoever it is for trying to interrupt me.

Trying to keep my cool I bite out, "Do you mind?"

His gloved hands are on my table, and I can sense he is leaning over me.

"As a matter of fact—"

I look up as the man slides into the spot vacated by Broc only moments before.

"Shit man, look, I'm not trying to start anything."

There sitting across from me is Terrance, Caston's head security. His face is tight as he clenches his jaw; his lips in a tight line.

His voice is cool and collected when he speaks. "I'm going to make this easy for you. Tell me what you are planning, tell me what Beverly is planning, and I'll make sure none of that happens. Once, you do, I'll give you two options. You can either chose to back off and disappear for good this time, or we can do things the hard way."

My eyes narrow. "You set this up with Broc?"

"You're a smart one." He chuckles.

A low growl forms in my chest. Who does this smug ass think he is?

"I wouldn't get all high and mighty with me. You know I have to capability of ending you for good."

He calls the waitress over with a flick of his wrist and orders a drink. Once she disappears, his eyes stare into mine. I'm suddenly no longer hungry and push the food away from me.

"So you just expect me to spill my guts to you in this public place?"

A smug look covers his face. "Doesn't seem so public to me."

Confused I begin to glace around. Everyone is gone. He emptied a busy restaurant. "Seriously?"

"Well, we could go to the police station, if you'd prefer."

My mouth goes dry. Shit. "I've gotta take a piss."

"Be my guest, but you can't escape, so don't even try."

Scrambling out of the booth, I take off toward the bathroom. Once inside, I lock the door behind me and lean against it, trying to calm my breathing.

Shit, shit, shit! What am I going to do? Give it up. Can I? I'm talking to myself as I pace the small room. I brace my hands on the sink and stare at myself in the mirror. Just when I am about to lose it my phone vibrates in my pocket. Fumbling to get it out, I turn it over and my heart clenches.

Kaitlyn: Hey, baby, just thinking about you. Hope you're being good. ;)

I smile thinking about her. What has come over me? Quickly, I type my response and head out the door.

Just thinking about any future with her, I know what I need to do.

Returning to my seat, I slide in and fold my arms over my chest. "Okay, where do you want me to start?

Chapter Twenty-Seven

Sabrina

I'm sitting staring at myself in the mirror. It's been five weeks since we've been back from Mexico and all I want to do is go back there. Caston and I were free. No work, no wedding planning, no responsibilities. Being an adult is for the birds. I look up to the ceiling and talk to my parents. *I wish you were here. Tomorrow is the biggest day of my life. I miss you so much.* Taking a few more minutes to myself before I grab my bag and head for the door to the bedroom. Beth insisted we stay at the hotel tonight because Caston can't see me until I walk down the aisle tomorrow. I fought her tooth and nail, arguing that it was an old wives tail. Nothing bad was going to happen. We've made it this far, we can make it through anything.

I grab the door knob, pulling the door toward me. My head is down, so I startle when I notice Caston standing there.

"Caston, you—"

He places his mouth over mine and stops my words with his kiss. I drop my bag and let my hands slide through his hair. Caston's arm hooks around my waist, pulling me into his hard chest. Backing me into the room, he shuts the door with his foot. I moan into his mouth as my insides clench.

Guiding me toward the bed, his devilish smile makes my knees go weak.

"Bre, I need you. I couldn't let you go without having you one last time as Ms. Bennett."

I grab the hem of his shirt and rip it up over his head.

"Mr. Black, I always need you."

I pull him toward me by his belt, slamming my mouth to his again. Fumbling with the metal of the buckle, I eventually get to the granite shaft begging to be set free. He groans into my mouth when I stroke it from base to tip. Feeling the bead of fluid form at the tip, I wipe it up with my finger and bring it up to my mouth. Sucking it, I watch him as he disposes of his pants and socks.

"Fuck, you taste good," I say as I pop my finger out of my mouth.

"Bre, I want to taste you." His voice is low and breathy.

I slowly pull my dress over my head. The shoes stay on. I know he likes to fuck me when I'm wearing heels. Stepping back, his eyes rake over my body.

"If I had known you weren't wearing panties, I would've taken you earlier," he growls.

Being a smart ass I ask, "Where exactly would you have done that? The back of the church, the Sunday school room? Oh how about the Preacher's waiting room?"

Growling, he pulls me into him and begins to trail his lips down my neck while his fingers roll my nipples into hard peaks. As his teeth graze my jaw, I once again let my hands slide into his silky hair. I can feel him between my legs. Squeezing my thighs together, gripping him tighter makes him pinch my nipples hard.

199

"Fuck, Caston." My voice is more of a breath.

He laughs into my neck between kisses. "I should've done you in all those places. Damn, I'm going to hell." I feel a small nip and pull away.

Giving him my serious face. "No marks. I have to wear this crazy white dress tomorrow, and I need to look virginal."

He pounces at me again, lifting me up into his strong arms.

"You are far from virginal."

I laugh. "That's why I said look."

Wrapping my legs around his waist, I let my heels dig into his ass. He slides into me. I'm ready for the abrupt action. Feeling him hard and deep in me, makes my head fall back. I soak in the feeling. He's slow at first, making me crazy.

"Caston, faster. Please, faster."

My chest raises and lowers quickly. His hands grip my ass, kneading it. He leans forward to place a kiss on the pale skin of my breast.

"Faster, huh?"

"Mmmm, please." I'm enjoying the slow motions, but I really need to be pounded.

I feel the skin on my breast start to ache, I know he's sucking. Marking me. Just as I was about to say something, he backs me up and slams me into the wall. His cock picks up speed, and I've lost all ability to form any words.

Pulling my ass, he spreads the cheeks apart. I'm completely open to him. His fingers slide closer together and one circles my ass. It causes my first orgasm to detonate around his cock. My hands are pulling his hair, scratching at his back, and gripping onto anything they can reach. Not stopping to let me recover, he picks up his pace once again, and I can feel another wave on the brink. I stretch my hands above my head, arching my back to push my body into him. Just when I think I can't have another orgasm his finger slides into my ass. The stretch and pinch sends a scream of ecstasy escaping me, making me clench him hard, and pushing me over that edge. I can't catch my breath. He follows me over the edge filling me with his hot come.

I bury my head in his neck and hold on as the ripples of my orgasms continue to detonate. I'm so completely relaxed, tears start to slip from my eyes.

Slowly letting my legs fall to the ground, he lifts my chin with his finger.

"Hey, why the tears? I didn't think it was that bad," He says, trying to bring light heartedness back to the moment.

I laugh through my tears. "I'm just so happy. All the emotions are just coming out."

A light kiss is placed on my lips, and I smile. "I love you so much it hurts, Caston. Sorry for the tears. It's just a very emotional time for a girl."

"I understand."

He holds me close until I calm down.

A while later, when we are both presentable again, Caston grabs my bags before reaching for my hand. "Ready."

I nod, and we head out the door to the stairs. The music and the chatter from the party downstairs celebrating our wedding rehearsal carries on as if the guests of honor weren't even missing.

"Glad to know we were missed."

Caston just laughs and places a kiss on the top of my head. "That's why I put on such fantastic parties."

I look at him confused. We reach the bottom of the steps and he sets my bag down and rest his hands on my hips. "Because then, my dear, we can sneak off anytime we want, and no one is the wiser."

Rising up on my toes, I lean into his ear. "I like when you sneak me off."

We're about to get lost in a kiss when Beth interrupts us.

Her perky voice travels over the chatter. "Ready to go?"

"No, I don't want to stay at the hotel."

She puts her hands on her hips, just as she is about to start arguing with me, Jake slides in next to her, placing his arm around her waist. I smile when I see her sink into his embrace. I know that feeling all too well. Caston squeezes me, so I know he saw the same thing I did.

"Maybe just give her a few more minutes, Elizabeth." He kisses her cheek and reaches for the bags by Caston's feet.

Beth's cheeks turn red at their interaction.

Knowing I'm just extending the inevitable, I kiss Caston's chest. "I should get going. Don't want to get to the hotel too late. I have this big thing happening tomorrow."

"I'll miss you." He scratches his chin. "I don't think I have anything tomorrow, might just spend the day in bed."

Beth's mouth hangs open, and I smack him lightly on the chest. "You better be there, mister."

"Oh I'll be there. I was thinking of going to sit on the steps of the church right now." Pulling me in for a tighter hug. He nuzzles my neck, making me giggle.

Jon walks up and shoves his way between us, swinging his arms around our shoulders.

"So, the ladies are going to the hotel, and I'm going to get Caston fucked up one last time in the name of bachelorhood."

I lean forward and glare at Caston. This was not the plan. He was smiling like a fool until he sees me looking at him.

"That's what you're doing? Maybe I should leave Jake to keep an eye on you."

Caston shakes his head. "No, baby, I'm not doing anything. I'm going to get all these people to leave, then I'm going to bed. A lonely, cold bed."

Beth reaches for me, pulling me out of Jon's embrace. "See, he's going to behave. Let's get going."

"Walk me to the car?" I produce my best puppy dog eyes.

He's reaching for my hand and pulling it up to his lips. "Of course, I wouldn't let you leave without getting a few more kisses in."

Beth just rolls her eyes. She grabs my purse and follows us out of the door to the waiting limo.

Chapter Twenty-Eight

Caston

Walking my love to the limo, I'm nervous because I haven't told her about all the new security threats we've been informed of. I have a security meeting with everyone as soon as Beth takes Bre to the hotel. I need to make sure our day goes off without a hitch. She's been so nervous, I don't want anything to go wrong. I hate having to lie to her.

One last kiss, then I shut the door, place my hands in my pockets, and watch the taillights of the limo until I can't see them anymore. Jon is once again at my side.

"Ready to get this show on the road?"

I just shake my head. "Why can't we just get rid of her for good?"

Jon smacks my back as we turn to head back into the house. "Oh we could, but then we'd be in jail for life. I don't know about you, but I don't think I could handle only having conjugal visits. I would hang myself."

Stopping in my tracks, I look at him. "Really, you're just thinking of your dick in this situation?"

He shrugs and walks off in front of me. I'm not sure how, but the house is mostly cleared of people and the cleaning crew is already fast at work to make sure I'll never know there was a party here. I loosen my tie and undo my cufflinks shoving them into my pocket. Walking toward the den, I roll up my sleeves and run my hands through my hair, ruffling it a bit.

Walking into the room the conversations stop and everyone focuses on me. "Evening, gentlemen and lady."

A round of pleasantries go around the room. "Let's get this show on the road. I'd like to make it to bed and get a few hours in before tomorrow."

"Very well, sir," Terrance begins. "As you all know we've had an in with Mark for the last few weeks. As much as I don't like to admit he is helping us, he has given us some valuable information pertaining to Beverly. I'm not sure he has given us all of his cooperation, unfortunately. I still believe there is something he is hiding which—"

"Is why we decided to make sure the guests were clean before they entered tomorrow." The redhead in the back speaks up.

"I'm sorry, I don't remember your name." I shift some papers around on my desk.

"Sorry, sir. It's Kaitlyn. Terrance hired me to be with Sabrina during more personal moments. I've also been the one that's gotten close to Mark, but he's very good at covering his tracks." A light blush appears on her cheeks.

"Ah, yes, I remember now. Go on."

"We sent everyone who RSVP'd a computerized card to bring with them in order to get access. When scanned at the check-in location it will bring up a picture of the guests to make sure no one had their card stolen and no one will be able to get in without that card."

Terrance takes over. "Sir, Kaitlyn has been undercover getting close with Mark for a few months now. He keeps telling Kaitlyn that as soon as he's done with his next job he'll be free. I really think we need to bring in metal detectors. Mark hasn't indicated in any way that he will be anywhere near the wedding, but we can't be sure. He only talks about his job, but we are unsure what that is exactly."

Concerned about my employee's well-being I ask, "Kaitlyn, Mark hasn't hurt you when you interacted with him right?"

She blushes again. I wonder what that reaction is about. "No, sir, he hasn't. Actually, besides a few outbursts, he seems like a totally different person than his file states. I'm shocked to see his record."

I nod. "Yes, unfortunately, monsters like Mark and Beverly are usually really good at hiding their past and have a tendency to snap. Terrance, I don't want metal detectors. I don't want to treat my guests like that."

Terrance just shakes his head and types something into his phone. I know we've had this conversation before, but I don't want to look back on my wedding day and remember metal detectors and gobs of security.

"So, the cops will be on standby, around the corner," Terrance continues. "We'll have men posted at each entrance, and no one can come in or leave through any door except the main entrance. Once Sabrina arrives, the side door will be locked."

I lean forward and rest my elbows on the desk. "Am I stupid for going through with this?"

No one answers me, not that I expected them too.

"Is there anything else?" I'm at my wits end.

"Bruce and a few other men are at the church sweeping it now. I will head over as soon as we finish up here," Terrance answers.

Nodding, I stand up and grab my phone from the desk. "Okay, thank you everyone for working overtime on this. No more mess ups.

We'll get them once and for all. Beverly and Mark will not hurt anyone again."

I walk out of the den and head toward my room. The house is quiet and dark now. Too quiet. I have too many thoughts and worries going through my head. The clock in the foyer chimes midnight. Smiling, I open my phone and send a text to Bre.

Today you will become Mrs. Black. I can't wait.

I throw the phone on the bed and strip down to my boxers. Crawling into bed, I think back to my life before Sabrina and how lonely it was. My phone chimes a return text.

Love you. I can't wait either. Now go to bed.

Smiling I quickly type back.

You aren't sleeping. Plus, I can't sleep when you aren't with me.

I can see she's typing back, so I wait for her response.

Me either. Beth snores. Will you still marry me with bags under my eyes?

Nothing would stop me from marrying you. Try to get some rest.

You too. XOXO

XOXOX

I set my phone down and send a silent prayer to her parents and all that is holy to watch over us tomorrow. Terrified isn't even the word to describe how I'm feeling. I know something is going to happen, I just don't know what or when.

Chapter Twenty-Nine

Sabrina

I shove Beth a little to try to quiet her. I forgot what it was like to sleep in the same room with her. She fell asleep watching a movie, and I was just too exhausted to try to move her. I remember why I couldn't wait for her to move out of our dorm to her apartment. She rolls over, but immediately pops out of bed, scaring the hell out of me.

"What the fuck?" I yell.

Her eyes are wide, and she runs to the bathroom. I shake my head and slide down under the covers trying to get comfy.

YES! I hear from inside the bathroom. Then the water runs and Beth appears in the doorway doing a little happy dance.

Propping my head up on my hand, I laugh. "Take it everything came out okay?"

She skips back to the bed and jumps in. "Bre, I've been so scared. I thought I was pregnant."

I sit straight up. "What?"

She slides back under the covers, pulling them up to her chest. "Ya, well, Jake and I had an 'oops' a few weeks ago. Then I was late. I had a test in my bag. I was going to take it in the morning, but looks like I won't need it now. Must have just been stress."

How is she trying to go back to bed right now? "Beth, why didn't you tell me?"

She shrugs. "You've been so stressed with this wedding, I didn't want to add anymore. Plus, even if I was I would still fit in my dress and all that, so it wouldn't interfere with anything."

My mouth hangs open. "No, but you can talk to me about anything."

"I know, but I don't need to now. Oh, I better text Jake. I think he was more worried than I was."

She sends off her text and rolls over to go back to bed. How is she so calm about this?

I slide back down and pull the covers up thinking about how I'll never have to worry about that. Tears form in my eyes. It's been a few months since my last period, but that isn't new. I think about the doctors telling me it was nearly impossible for me to conceive after all that happened to me with my last pregnancy. I fall asleep crying.

My alarm goes off, and I feel as though I just shut my eyes. I reach out and smack my phone to snooze. I roll onto my back and stretch. Just then a jolt goes through my body. I'm getting married in a few hours. My stomach turns, but I ignore it and I shake Beth. "Time to get up."

She rolls over, placing the pillow over her head. "No, too early."

"I know, but we have hair and makeup coming in about forty-five minutes."

She turns her head to look at me. "Then that gives me forty-five more minutes of sleep. Leave me alone."

Shaking my head, I swing my legs over the side of the bed and walk toward the bathroom. Just as I am about to close the door, I see

Beth's bag on the chair. Remembering what she said about the pregnancy test, I tiptoe over to her bag and move a few things to see if she really has one with her. Sure enough, there it is staring back at me.

I'm frozen. Why am I even considering taking it? I know it'll be negative, and I'll be crushed. I know there's no chance of me being pregnant. Not only because I've been taking my pill, but... I let the thought trail off. Wringing my hands in front of me, I chomp down on my lip. Grabbing it quickly, I take off toward the bathroom, shutting the door behind me and locking it.

I set the test on the counter. Walking over to the shower, I turn it on to get nice and steamy. I run my hands through my hair. My mind is devoid of any thoughts, and I'm completely calm. I wonder if that's strange for someone who's getting married in a few hours. Out of the corner of my eye that box catches my attention again. Undressing for the shower, I decide to just do it.

After taking the test, I chicken out before seeing the result. I throw the test and the box in a drawer in the vanity. Out of sight out of mind. I step into the shower and wash up. Just before I am about to get out, I hear banging on the door.

"Come on, Bre, you've been in there forever. Stacie, Andrea, Julia, and Rachel are here for our hair and makeup."

I step out of the shower, wrapping myself in a towel. "I'll be right out. Did Sara show up yet?"

"Yes, waiting on you," she says a little annoyed.

I just laugh. It's my wedding and they have to wait for me. "Be out in a minute. Can you send Sara in for a sec?"

"Ugh, fine. Hurry, okay?"

I slip my robe on and use the towel on my hair. Fluffing it up, so the curls don't turn to frizz. There's a quiet knock on the door.

"Bre?"

Walking over to the door, I open it to allow Sara to come in. We haven't talked much since Mexico, and I need to clear the air with her.

She glances down before walking into the steamy room. Shutting the door behind her, I immediately pull her in to a huge hug. She tenses at my embrace.

"Sara, I don't want it to be like this with us. I'm sorry for how I reacted. I was confused and scared."

She pulls back and frowns a bit. "We've been together before."

I motion for her to sit on the edge of the whirlpool while I continue to work on my hair. "I know, but Caston was always with me. I let my feelings take over, but my subconscious put me in check. If he isn't with me, it's cheating, Sara."

"No, it isn't. We've been together before, so it isn't."

I walk over to her and sit. "Sara, Caston and I don't have the same kind of relationship that you and Jon have. We only want to be together. Yes, we occasionally do multiples, but he's always with me, and he's the only guy that I want to be with. That's the way I want it to be."

Sara looks at me confused.

"That doesn't mean we can't be together again, but you and I can't be intimate together, alone," I further explain.

She nods.

"Can we be good again? I miss you."

She lunges at me, arms open. "Bre, I've missed you so much. I'm so sorry I pushed you. I hope we can be together again soon, but I understand and respect your relationship with Caston. I won't push again."

Tears are running down both of our faces. I squeeze her. We finally part and wipe our eyes with the backs of our hands.

"Let's get this out of our system now. I don't want to be puffy for my wedding day."

She laughs through the tears. My robe parts a little showing some of my breast.

"My God, Bre, what the hell did Caston do to you?" She pulls open the top further.

Looking down, I turn toward the mirror. Bastard marked me three times on my breasts last night. "Damn, him. I told him not too. I hope it doesn't show with my dress on, or Rachel is going to have a fun time trying to cover them."

She comes up behind me and snaps a picture. "I'm sending this to Caston to yell at him."

I turn around with my mouth open. He's not supposed to see me before the wedding. She smiles with a devilish grin. "No worries, your face isn't in it."

I just laugh and head for the door. Her text chime returns. Stopping, I turn around to see what he said.

"He told me to tell you he did one for the past, present, and future."

I place my hand on the door knob. "Well, isn't he charming?" We both start laughing.

Sara starts to walk toward me, but her shorts catch on the vanity drawer knob. Her first step pulls the drawer out, making it crash to the floor.

"Shit."

I rush to her side and start grabbing at the box and stick.

"Whoa, is that what I think that is?" She stops and looks up at me.

Sara grabs it out of my hand before I can do anything with it. Then the words fly out of my mouth before even thinking. "It's Beth's."

Chapter Thirty

Sabrina

The girls slide my dress over my head and it falls into place. Perfect fit. I can see Beth start to tear up.

"No, don't. Please, don't start."

She bites her lip and sniffles. "I can't help it. You're gorgeous."

Sara finishes zipping me into the dress and smooths it out. "There, perfect."

I look over my shoulder and catch her eye. She has tears in them too.

Beth reaches over and grabs my shoes while Sara leaves to grab my veil. Pulling her dress up, she kneels before me to help me into them. I have an overwhelming feeling of being Cinderella as I hold my foot out for her to slip my shoe on.

"Veil, then we are done," Sara says, walking in from the other room.

The palms of my hands are starting to sweat. I start wringing them in front of me. Beth reaches out and grabs them. "No fidgeting. You're beautiful, you have a wonderful guy, you are one lucky bitch, do you know that?"

I squeeze her hands and pull her to me and wrap her in a big hug. Sara stops in the doorway, giving us a minute, but I wave her over. She has helped me get to this perfect moment too. The smile that spreads on her face makes me so happy. She joins in on the embrace.

"Thank you, girls. Really, I wouldn't be here if it wasn't for you two."

We all part, and Sara slides the veil into my hair. Beth dabs her eyes. "Are you ready?" she asks me.

I take a deep breath. "I think so," I whisper.

Sara smiles. "Turn around, honey. You're so beautiful."

Taking another deep breath, I turn slowly. My breath catches as I see myself for the first time and tears start falling.

"Wow."

Beth and Sara nod behind me.

Standing before me is a grown women, ready to embark on the most terrifying, most amazing journey of her life. I can't help but think that my mom should be with me right now helping me get dressed and my dad should be standing in the corner waiting for his little girl.

I let my arms smooth my dress at the sides. The drop waist lace dress was perfect. I knew it the moment I saw it a few months back. The layers of lace that fall to the floor are light but full. The train isn't too long, but it's perfect. I pull up my dress to see my shoes. The white shoes with crystalized heels and blue soles were absolutely perfect, elegant and sexy. I reach up to touch my necklace. Caston. All of this is for him, and I can't wait to see him.

Beth takes this moment to hand me a hankie. I dab my eyes, trying not to mess up my makeup. My hair is pulled up with a few tendrils falling out. The cathedral length veil is the perfect complement to my dress. I'm ready.

"Oh, I almost forgot." Sara rushes out of the room.

She comes back carrying a small blue bag. "Caston asked me to give this to you."

Dabbing my eyes again, I reach for the bag. I take it out of the bag and gasp. "Oh my God. How?"

Sara shrugs. Beth tries to see what I'm holding. I turn around and hold it out for her to see. Her hand flies up to her mouth.

"Sara, how did he get this?"

"It's Caston, sweetie. How he does anything is a mystery to me."

I clasp my shaky hand around my mother's wedding ring. It's the most beautiful rose gold with three little pink diamonds on the band. I'd recognize this ring anywhere. It was unlike any I've ever seen. It fit her perfectly. I remember telling Caston about the day she showed up without it one afternoon we were snuggling on the couch.

I'd just gotten done practicing and *Claire De Lune* was playing in the background. She was nervously rubbing her ring finger. *'Mom where's your ring?'* I asked her.

'Oh, it's nothing, honey. No worries.'

I could tell that wasn't the truth. I gathered my bags, but kept my eye on her. Her eyes were puffy and red. They were glassy, like she could cry at any minute.

'Mom, please tell me.'

She looked up at me from the seat she had taken. *'Oh honey, I sold it. We needed the money and Joe had been asking me about it for a while. He said he never saw anything like it before. I got a lot of money for it.'*

I couldn't believe what she just said. I sat next to her and grabbed her hand in mine. *'Mom, why?'*

She just shook her head and tears began to fall again. *'So you can dance,'* she whispered.

I slide the ring onto my finger and pull out his note.

Your something old. I've been keeping this for a while and knew today was the perfect day to give it to you. You need a piece of your parents with you today and what better than your mother's wedding ring, the symbol of your parents's love? They would be so proud of you. I can't wait to see you at the end of the aisle. I love you, Bre

Thank you for making me whole.

Love always,

Caston

I place my hand over my stomach and cry. How am I going to make it through today without them? My parents should be here to give me away. Sara and Beth guide me to a chair.

I'm on the verge of hyperventilating. "I'm so sorry," I choke out between sobs.

"No apologies." Beth pulls me in for a big hug. "Honey, you have to breathe. No trips to the hospital today, okay?"

Nodding, I wipe at my eyes again. Rachel and Julia walk into the room with a big sheet. "Okay, everyone out. We have to make her look as though she wasn't just crying her eyes out."

We all laugh through our tears. "Hope that's all for the night," I say.

A short time later I appear in the main room. Sara and Beth have been joined by Terrance and Kaitlyn.

"Are you ready, Sabrina?" Terrance asks.

"Yes, more than ready."

"Wait!" Beth announces, stopping us in the doorway. "The six pence."

"What?" I ask.

"You know something old, your mom's ring. Something new, your dress. Something borrowed, my hankie. I want that back after you wash it, of course. Something blue, the soles of your shoes. Lucky six pence in your shoe."

She produces a coin from her pocket book and lifts my dress up, pulling my foot towards her. Sara grabs my arm to help steady me.

"Well, this is going to be uncomfortable."

She looks up at me. "Just until after the ceremony. Okay, now you're all set."

Looking over to Terrance, I giggle. "I guess, now, I'm more than ready."

He just chuckles and shakes his head. Beth hands me my bouquet of pure white roses with red berries poking through. We all head out the door. Terrance and Kaitlyn in front, Sara and I, Beth carrying my train, and then Jake.

We walk outside to jump into the waiting limo. It's a beautiful day. The sun is shining, with a light breeze. The leaves are the brightest shades of yellow, orange, and red.

Arriving at the church, I walk into the vestibule and can hear Bach's "Air on the G String" playing. I know this was the last song before the girls head down the aisle. It's almost time.

Looking around, I see men in tuxes everywhere with ear pieces in. Things move in slow motion, but the music stays the correct tempo. It's surreal. Sara and Beth are laughing. Julia is there putting a few extra pins in my hair. One last dash of powder on my nose and Rocco, the wedding coordinator, is lining everyone up like we'd planned last night.

Pachelbel's "Canon in D" starts. The doors to the church open. You can hear the benches creak as everyone turns to look toward the back.

Sara takes her place in the doorway, turning back, she blows me a kiss. Jake holds his arm out, and Sara takes it walking toward the altar. A few seconds later Beth takes her place and heads out the door alone. The coordinator is behind me, holding my dress and veil up. I wait for the music change. It's almost as if I've done this a million times.

The doors close again, and I take my place behind them, alone. Caston asked if I wanted anyone to walk me down the aisle. I couldn't fathom someone taking my dad's place. Even though he isn't here physically, I feel him standing next to me. The air flies around me as my dress is fluffed. Everyone seems to scatter and as the first few chords of "Trumpet Voluntary" start, the doors swing open and everyone stands. For me. *I'm ready, Daddy, are you?* I count to three and start my walk down the aisle.

It's then that I see him. Waiting for me. My future husband. My love. My life. I can see nothing but him. He's wearing a black tux with a crisp white shirt, white vest, and white tie. He's never looked so good. His smile lights up the room. I see him wipe his eye and a tear slides down my cheek too.

Reaching the end of the aisle, I blow out a breath as Caston reaches for my hand. He raises my hand up to his lips.

"You look beautiful," he whispers and another tear falls down my cheek. His other hand comes up and wipes it away.

"Ready?" he asks.

I glance over to the empty pew that was left for my parents. I can almost see them there smiling at me. Looking back at Caston, I smile. "Ready."

He helps me walk the last few feet up a few stair steps to the priest. The music ends and the ceremony begins.

Chapter Thirty-One

Caston

I take my place at the altar with Jon by my side. I'm trying to shake the funny feeling I've had all morning. Today will be perfect, one way or another. I smile at Sara when she makes her way to the front of the church. She sends me a wink, then I focus on Beth next. Once Sara and Beth are in their places, there's a short pause.

The music changes and the doors open. I'm at a loss for words when I see her appear in the doorway of the church. All I can see is Sabrina. She looks radiant. There's a glow about her, like an angel. I feel like we're the only two people in this church. Tears escape, and I wipe them away. I don't think anything can ruin this moment for us.

She finally reaches my side. This is where she belongs. Forever. I pull her hand to my mouth, placing a kiss on her mom's ring. I'm so glad I could do that for her. Her tears fall again, and I wipe them away with my thumb as I caress her face.

Once we make it to the priest, we both take a deep breath, face each other as the priest begins.

"Dearly beloved, we are gathered here today, to join Sabrina

Marie Bennett and Caston Michael Black in holy matrimony, which is not by any to be entered into unadvisedly or lightly, but reverently, discreetly, advisedly and solemnly."

Sabrina looks at me and makes a face that makes me chuckle. The priest pauses looking at me sideways. Bre squeezes my hands, and I look at her and smirk back. I shake my head lightly. I can't believe she's making me laugh when we're supposed to be serious. Another reason why I love her.

"Sorry," I whisper to the priest.

He clears his throat and continues, "Into this holy estate these two persons present now come to be joined. If any person can show just cause why they may not be joined together, let them speak now or forever hold their peace."

The part I've been dreading. I hold my breath, and I squeeze Bre's hands. Her eyes are closed. She doesn't like this part either. I feel like the priest is pausing longer than normal.

Commotion at the back of the church pulls everyone's attention.

"Fuck," I mutter.

Chapter Thirty-Two

Mark

I pace nervously outside of the church. After talking with Terrance at the diner, I wasn't sure if this would still be happening. I thought for sure he would somehow figure out my plans, even though I managed to stay away from talking about them. I told him about Beverly's plan for sabotage down to the very last detail. Since, my plan's almost in full swing, I have just a few more small details, and it'll finally be done. The alleyway outside of the church is dark. Where the fuck is Bruce?

Pulling out my phone, I check the time. It's almost midnight. Almost D-day. A noise makes me flatten myself up against the stone exterior of the church. The door swings open and Bruce walks out.

"Mark?"

I step out of the shadows. Pulling the hood up on my sweatshirt, I walk over to him.

"Whatcha got for me?"

Bruce looks around nervously before looking back at me. Pulling out a cigarette, he lights up and takes a deep drag before beginning.

He slowly passes me a card.

"This is what you'll need to get in. They decided against metal detectors, so you won't have to leave anything here tonight. If anything changes, I'll contact you."

Nodding, I slide the card in my pocket. "Does everything still seem to be the same?"

"Ya, Sabrina's going to the hotel. Caston's at home. Terrance should be here any minute to sweep the church again. Bastard is so paranoid." He laughs deep and it bounces around the alleyway.

Grabbing the cigarette, I pull the smoke deep into my lungs feeling it calm me. Blowing it out, I throw the butt on the ground and crush it with my foot.

"See you tomorrow." I clap him on the shoulder and take off down into the darkness.

A few short hours later, I'm standing in my room adjusting my tux. Beverly has made herself scarce, and her room has been cleared out. I haven't seen her in a week, and I question myself if I should still go through with this. I grab my phone and press the button bringing the screen to life. Kaitlyn's face shines back at me. My insides felt warm thinking that soon I will be meeting up with her to start my new life, but I know if I don't finish this the bitch will haunt me for the rest of my life until it's done.

Donning my jacket, I grab my guns. Here we go.

Arriving at the church, the hustle and bustle of the guests is nerve wrecking. I stick to myself and try not to look at anyone in the eye. I pat my pocket and feel the card that Bruce gave me last night. Since I haven't heard from him, I hope to hell it works or everything will be over before I even start.

The church bells begin ringing. Looking up to the sky, it's a beautiful sunny day. Standing in line, I fidget with my jacket to make sure everything is covered. The girls in front of me are chattering away when one of them looks at me.

"Are you a friend of the bride or groom?" Her southern drawl's so thick it was almost hard to understand her.

"Um." Making eye contact, I recognize her as Hollywood Sweetheart of the Year from two years ago. Her friend links her arm and smiles at me. I shake my head when I remember they're waiting for me to answer. "Bride. Known her since college."

They sigh and place their hands on their chests as we move closer to the door. "Isn't she just the luckiest? Caston is so amazing. Wish it was me he fell in love with. Can't say I didn't try." The girls start laughing, and I roll my eyes and glance backwards.

Thankfully, we're at the front of the line, and I can already hear the music playing. Perfect timing. I just hope there's a seat at the back. The girls make it in with no problem. Quickly handing the card to the guy at the door. He scans the plastic thing and taps the screen a few times. Seconds seem to last for hours.

"You may proceed, sir. Thank you."

Nodding, I quickly walk from the check-in area through the maze of halls into the church vestibule. I'm immediately hit with the floral smell of the decorations, and I hear voices coming from around the corner, recognizing Beth's. Feeling the pit in my stomach drop, I duck into the church and take my seat on the end of a pew toward the back.

I make it in just in time to see the doors close and the music changes. The chatter slows, Caston and Jon walk out, taking their place up front. The room is lined with security with ear pieces. Stretching my neck, I peer toward the front of the church and immediately find Terrance. Smirking, since he isn't looking at me, good, because he would immediately end this whole thing. Just as Terrance turns his head, I think my cover will be blown, people shift their attention to the back again, and the doors open.

I recognize Sara, Caston's sister-in-law, walking down the aisle. When she gets to the middle, she joins up with her escort. My collar tightens, Jake, the trainer from the gym, what the fuck was he doing here? I feel the sweat form on my brow as I watch them make their way to the front. Turning back around, Beth is making her way down. When she gets close, I glance away, so Beth doesn't see me and ruin everything.

Second thoughts are once again flooding my brain, I don't have to do this. Maybe I shouldn't. The music changes again, and I look at the doors opening. There she is. Sabrina looks beautiful, happy. Her eyes are locked on Caston at the front of church. My heart clenches at how horrible I was to her.

I can't bring myself to turn away now. If she sees me, I know it will be over, but she won't. I don't think she's seeing anyone or anything right now. I wonder if it will be like this for Kaitlyn and me. I hope so, I want to find happiness.

Once she reaches the front, I see Caston wipe her tears. He took her away from me. I need them out of my life forever. I could have been her forever. Then again, I would have never met Kaitlyn.

A smile creeps up on my face when I day dream of us up on that alter. I can just picture her with her red hair up with some falling around her face, like it does when she puts it up. The white dress and veil. I bet my vixen would have a tight simple dress through. She isn't into frill. Damn her body would fucking rock in a dress like that.

As I'm daydreaming, I realize that the cue I was waiting for is upon me. That one line in every wedding that no one likes. Objections? HA! It's the cruelest line in the wedding. Some sick fuck had to have come up with it, but I fucking love it.

Placing my hands on my guns, I suddenly realize I don't want to do this. I want to let them live the rest of their lives in peace and so do

I. I step out into the aisle, tripping on the runner before getting my footing. A few people turn to look in my direction at the small distraction I caused. I see some security guards reaching for their ear piece. Shit! Hope they don't recognize me.

I'm almost to the doors when, gasps from the guests to my right start a commotion, causing the entire church to shift its attention in that direction.

"I fucking new it. I knew you didn't have the balls!" The screech of her voice cracks through the silence. She continues pushing her way through the crowd. I see it then. The gun reflects in the sun from the stained glass window.

"Mark, you'll never be anything. You can't do one simple task. This would have been over with already if you didn't fuck up the first time."

"Beverly, no! No more." Changing my direction from the exit to try to get to her.

"STOP!" she screams, cocking her gun and shooting it into the air. "She goes with me and no one gets hurt."

The screams that radiate through the church echo off the stone walls. Looking over to Caston, I see him instinctively move Sabrina behind him to protect her. Stupid son of a bitch, she'll kill them both.

I hear the clicks of guns being chambered all around me.

"Call them off, Caston," she seethes pointing the gun directly at his chest. Sabrina lets out a whimper.

"You don't scare me, Beverly," he says much too calmly.

"You should be scared."

"I'm not fucking around, Caston. Hand her over." She makes a gesture with her hand, indicating she wants him to pass Sabrina to her.

"Beverly, you don't want her. Don't ruin their lives." My voice tries to stay calm and collected as I make my way closer to her.

That's when my life snaps me back to reality. I hear her.

"Mark?" I look around me franticly. No way is she here. How is she here? Kaitlyn comes around the corner into my eyesight.

Suddenly my tough guy exterior is gone. The crack in my exterior has been ripped wide open. "Kaitlyn? Wha... what are you doing here?"

She slowly walks toward me. Her eyes are warm and full of love. For me, not Caston, not some other guy, me. Her smile is bright, but she's worried.

"This her," Beverly snaps, "your whore?"

Gritting my teeth I pull my own gun and yell, "Don't call her that!"

Security is moving in faster now to circle me now. Beverly's head falls back, emitting an evil laugh that echoes through the church.

Kaitlyn has reached my side and slides her arm around my waist reaching up on her toes to whisper in my ear, "Mark, don't do it. Pass the gun to me slowly and everything will be okay."

I glance down to her and let her other hand slowly slide down my arm lowering my gun toward the ground. Once her hand is on mine, she removes it from my hand and passes it behind her to Terrance.

Once my gun is gone, I wrap my arms around her, pulling her to my body. Heavy sobs wrack me. She reciprocates the hug and lets me hold her.

"You're so damn weak! My God! Does any man in my life have balls?" Beverly screams before lifting her gun and turning it in the direction of Kaitlyn and me, knowing she won't be reasoned with I snap, breaking free of Kaitlyn's hold, I take off toward Beverly.

She isn't looking at me though, she's looking behind me. Just as I make it to her, the gun goes off. I glance back and see Kaitlyn take a direct hit to the chest. Lunging the last few feet, I grab her gun and tackle her to the ground.

"NO!" An unrecognizable voice comes from me as I wrestle her. I feel the cold metal in my hands, and we roll so she is under me. The barrel is at my chest. Ripping it from her hands, I turn the vile thing back to her and let off one shot. Right through her heart. She won't get away with this. No more.

The gun falls to the side of me, and I place my hands on my head. Tears are falling down my face. It's over. I have nothing.

Just as I'm being shoved to the ground with men pulling my arms behind my back, I see her. Kaitlyn sits up with the help of Terrance. How? I saw her go down.

She looks toward me and gives me a sympathetic smile as Terrance opens her jacket, revealing her vest as he checks for other injuries. My heart breaks, realizing she's been in on this the whole time. I'm pulled to my feet by the officer when Terrance and Kaitlyn walk up to me.

"I thought you were dead. I couldn't take losing you. I love you." As the saddest possibility occurs, I whisper, "Was any of it real?"

She places her hand on my cheek, stroking her thumb back and forth. Terrance has her braced against him because she is unsteady from getting the wind knocked out of her. She can't say anything, but I see a flicker in her eyes before he pulls her to be checked out by the paramedics that just arrived.

My eyes flick over to the alter, Caston has Sabrina on his lap, cradling her against his chest. "I'm so sorry. Sorry for everything. Please, forgive me," I whisper as they pull me toward the door.

Chapter Thirty-Three

Caston

Watching everything unfold before us was crazier than any movie I've ever seen. Jake was trying to get me and Bre to the pastor's room for safety, but we were frozen in place. I'd never believe it if I hadn't seen it with my own eyes. She's gone, out of our lives forever, finally, and not because my men took her down. Mark of all people was the one to do it.

I pull Sabrina toward me, up into my arms. She isn't crying, she's devoid of any emotion. I hear Mark apologizing to us as they drag him out of the room. Sabrina tenses at the sound of his voice. Things are surreal, like I'm in a movie. Kaitlyn is being attended too, and Beverly's body is being covered with a cloth.

After hours of questioning and information, the officers finally clear us to leave the scene. Since Terrance is still working with them, Jake ushers us out the side door toward the hotel.

Once inside our room, I lay her on the bed. I crawl in behind her, pulling her to my chest. I just hold her. She begins to shake, and I know the events are finally sinking in. Repeatedly I kiss her soft hair.

Even though there's disorder in our suite, I don't move.

"Shhh, Bre. I'm here. We're safe. No one can hurt us anymore. Finally, we're free."

Her shoulders shake and she rolls to face me. She looks up into my eyes. Her eyes are puffy and red. I place a hand on her cheek.

"Are you sure?" she whispers.

I take a deep breath. Finally, I can answer and know for sure the answer. "Yes, baby. I'm sure."

Tears begin to run down her face, and she snuggles into my chest. We lay for hours together.

A few weeks have passed. We've been busy with police visits, statements of what happened, the arraignment of Mark, and press of all sorts. Mark finally spilled everything. He explained that he was the one that originally shot Sabrina, and he was also the one that kidnapped Sara and Jon. That's why the bullet didn't match Beverly's gun when they did forensics, and why they couldn't find any sort of DNA from Beverly on Sara and Jon when they were examined. He's been doing her dirty work, since he was kicked off the football team and lost his shot at the pros. Beverly sought him out and paid him very well.

Terrance was furious that he got in the church. He wasn't sure how it could have happened. Mark cleared that up for us too. Bruce was working with him and apparently he was also doing side work for Beverly, that's how she got in as well. Mark swore on his life he had no idea Bruce was working with her too. From what I saw I believed him, but I felt sick. That bastard was in my home. Saw personal items and was in on personal calls. Most importantly he probably told Beverly Rose was alive. FUCK!

Terrance immediately turned in his resignation to me, upon finding out about of Bruce's involvement. He felt it was his fault and something that would have been avoided if he caught it. I, however, wouldn't take it. He's done so much for me over the years, I couldn't just let him go. I've promoted Jake to be Sabrina's personal security. He'd told me he was leery about Bruce from the beginning, but I'd dismissed it because Terrance assured me that he was clean and had the background check come back fine.

Yesterday we got a call from Detective Alverez. He said that Mark asked for a private meeting with Sabrina and me. Of course, I wanted nothing to do with him. Sabrina, the sweetheart that she is, said she thought we should meet with him. Upon questioning her further she said she needed it to heal. To put it in the past. I reluctantly agreed.

I couldn't believe how strong she was when we walked into that room. They brought Mark in cuffed with his orange jumpsuit. Taking a seat, we all stared at each other for a few seconds in silence.

"You asked for this meeting, what do you want, Mark?" she started. I pulled her hand into my lap and held on to her tight. She looked down at our connection and smiled.

Upon seeing how happy we are, Mark sighed. "I just wanted to tell you to your face I'm sorry. Really sorry for everything. I turned into Ric, and that's everything I didn't want to do."

She nodded. "I can't say you're any better than him."

"I know. I'm sure you will never forgive me, but please know that I'm truly sorry. I just want what I see going between you two, real love. I thought I finally found that with Kaitlyn."

Sabrina just laughed. "Mark, I hope you find happiness someday. I don't think I will ever forgive you, but thank you." She moved to get up and I stood behind her.

"Caston," Mark stops me. "I don't have to tell you this, but take care of her."

I nod. I shouldn't say it, but I actually felt a little bad for him.

"Mark, Kaitlyn does feel those things for you." I had to tell him the truth. He should get some peace. After everything we've learned about him and his childhood, I have a little empathy for the things he endured at the hands of his step-father.

After that day, it's felt as though a ton of bricks was lifted from us.

Once I get word that we shouldn't be needed until the trial starts, I decide to sweep Sabrina off to Mexico.

Pulling Sabrina into my lap on the plane, I still can't believe all that has happened. We still aren't married. After Mark was taken into custody, the church was a crime scene, so we couldn't continue with the wedding. I wouldn't have wanted to remember our wedding like that anyways. Sabrina hasn't said anything about the wedding unless she's asked. I think it's her way of dealing with all the crazy. She has been using the studio more. I've even seen her with her pointe shoes on a few times.

"What's that silly smile for?" She asks when she looks up at me. Her big hazel eyes sparkle. There's so much life in them now that the air is cleared and all the threats are gone.

"Just thinking how we didn't give up and let those assholes split us up."

A smile engulfs her face and she leans in, grazing my lips with a chaste kiss. "I love you, Caston."

I shift her so she's straddling my lap. Taking her face in my hands, I return the kiss, deepening it. Finally parting, I rest my forehead on hers. "Bre, I love you more than you will ever know."

I hug her to my chest, and we just hold on to each other.

When we land in Mexico, Bre is peacefully asleep on my chest. Terrance appears in the cabin to let me know that we're ready to go.

"Is everything all set?"

He smiles. "Yes, sir."

"Bre, wake up honey we're here." I shift her slowly, so I don't startle her.

Her eyes flutter, and she moves to get up, but I pull her back into me. I wrap my arms around her and kiss her. She leans back, looking at me quizzically.

"Why are you smiling so big?"

"Just happy we are finally going to be married," I tell her.

She bounces up and down on my lap. "Caston, really? Here?"

I help her off my lap and stand up. Holding out my hand to her, she takes it and follows me off the plane.

A while later, we pull up to the house. I lean over to her ear. "Go change and meet me on the beach in half an hour. Sara and Beth packed a dress for you in this bag."

She giggles and takes off toward the bedroom. I set our bags down. Walking through the house, I slide my shoes off and roll up my khakis before stepping into the sand. The preacher greets me, and I inform her Sabrina should be out shortly.

No sooner did I say that than she appears in the doorway. Her hair is loose, and she has a simple white linen slip dress on. It skims her curves perfectly. The front is modest, but the back is low cut. Sliding off her sandals when she gets to the sand, she walks toward me with the biggest grin on her face.

Her hand slides into mine, and we face the preacher. This is how it should be, just us.

The preacher starts talking, and I can barely hear her, I'm so focused on Sabrina and how stunning she is.

"Your vows?" the preacher questions, bringing me out of my daydream. "Would you like me to do the traditional ones?"

I look over at Sabrina. "I'd like to say my own if that's okay with you, Bre?"

"But I didn't write any—"

I place a finger over her beautiful lips to quiet her.

She looks at me, the sun is setting behind her, and she's so damn beautiful. She doesn't have to say anything to me. I just want to remember her right now in this moment.

"Sabrina, from that first night I saw you, you captured my heart. It was yours, and I didn't even know who you were. Then we met, and you were in trouble. I thank God every day I was there to save you."

Tears start welling up in her eyes. Grabbing her hands, I squeeze them.

"You are my now and forever. I can't think of anyone else I'd want to spend my life with. Have I told you I love you? I do. More than you will ever know, and I will continue to tell you every day until we're parted by death. You saved me from the craziness, I'm a better man because of you. We didn't give up when times got rough, and I won't give up on anything with you by my side."

The tears start to trickle down her face. I pull a handkerchief from my pocket and wipe them away. She laughs through the tears.

"I promise I will always wipe away your tears. We're in this marriage together, good times, bad times, and okay times. I will be your strength, no matter what life throws at us. The future is bright, and I can't wait to see what is next for us."

I pull her hands up to my lips and gently kiss her palms. "Sabrina, this is my vow to you. I promise you."

Looking over at the preacher, I nod. She looks over to Sabrina for her to begin.

She takes a deep breath and begins in a whisper, "I love you, Caston. You are my knight in shining armor. We've been through so much in the short time we've been together, more than most will in a life time. We've made it through and we'll continue to make it. My love is yours. God knows we're worth it. Our future is bright. I'll continue to dance for you."

A huge smile spreads across my face. "I can't wait," I whisper.

"I give you my heart and my word that I won't give up. Good times and bad, sickness and health. I will never give up on us. You are my forever and always."

Finally we are husband and wife! Kissing her like it's the first time, there are claps behind us. Still embracing, we turn to look toward the house. Sara, Jon, Beth, Jake, Jules, and Terrance are all standing on the back patio. The girls are wiping away tears.

Then I see the movement in the dark corner beyond the crew, Rose and James. I pull Sabrina closer and smile. They made it. When I extended the invite to James he wasn't sure if he could talk her into it. Rose is here and the smile on her face makes me know we will be the family I have dreamed of.

"How?" Sabrina asks.

I pull her into a kiss again. Deepening it into a low dip as the cat calls continue. She giggles as I pull her upright again.

Smirking. "You know I have my ways."

She tisk tisks and shakes her head. "You are too much."

I pull her to me again, kissing my wife. "Bre, I'm so happy. Thank you. You make the rest of my life something to look forward too. Just us. Forever."

She smirks pulling away slightly. "Caston, I don't think I'd be alive right now if it wasn't for you. You make me whole. But…"

Her sentence trails off and she looks out over the ocean. I take her chin in between my fingers. "But what, Bre?"

"But it's not going to be just us for long."

My heart stops. Is she telling me what I think she is telling me? "What?"

She takes my hands in hers and she places them on her stomach. "It's going to be you, me, and baby." Tears start falling down her cheeks, but I know they're happy tears.

I fall to my knees and grab her hips before placing a soft kiss on her still flat tummy. A tear falls from my eyes.

"How?" I look up at her.

"Last time we were here, the time change didn't agree with my pill. I guess it was meant to be?" She shrugs, before more tears fall from her eyes.

"Are you sure?" I ask.

She nods. "Dr. Dana confirmed it a few days ago. I was waiting for the perfect moment to tell you."

I stand up and sweep her off her feet before spinning her around. We get lost in each other's kiss. Life is just getting started for us.

Epilogue

Sabrina

It's been four wonderful years, since I said 'I do' on this beach to the love of my life. Here we are again to celebrate our anniversary. Our life has been crazy since then. In a good way, of course.

Once Caston found out I was pregnant, he told everyone. If he could have gone door to door telling the world, I honestly think he would have. When we walked up to the house to join our friends and family, Caston spilled the news immediately. Beth's mouth fell open, and Sara screamed almost tackling us to the ground. I still chuckle thinking about it.

"You told me it was Beth's test, I'm so mad at you." Sara squeezed.

Beth's face lights up, like everything fell into place. Turning to Sara, she says, "So that's why you kept asking me if I should be drinking?"

I twist my hair. "Sorry. I was dumbfounded when I turned that test over and saw it was positive. I blurted out the first thing that came to my mind. Technically, it was your test, though."

Sara flips between looking at me and Beth. For once we caught her speechless.

I'm brought back to the present when I hear the footsteps of my little girl come bounding up the steps.

"Mommy—Daddy and I built a huge castle. Come on!" She grabs my hand, leading me to the beach. I smile at Cass, who's waiting down at the bottom of the steps.

"Don't pull on Mommy, Brianna," he says, reaching his hand up for me to take after a few steps.

My belly is round and full. I'm a lot bigger than I was with Brianna at this point.

He leans over and kisses my cheek. "How are you feeling, Bre? Did you get that nap?"

Our hands lace together as we follow my mini me down the beach toward the ocean. "I got a few winks. I was thinking back over the last four years."

He looks at me over the top of his sunglasses. "It's been a journey, hasn't it?"

I chuckle. "Mommy, Mommy, look."

We reach the monster castle, where Brianna stands by it with her hands on her hips. "Wow, you and Daddy did this whole thing?"

She nods enthusiastically. Going on to point out the little flags made out of sticks and seaweed, the windows made of sea shells, and the moat that goes around it.

"This is perfect, baby girl. I think you should build us a house." I scoop her off the ground. "Now, let's get back to the house. We have guests coming any minute."

She squeals as Caston grabs her from me, tickling her as she goes into his arms. "Daddy, stop." Her hair flying all around.

I can't help but tear up at the sight. "You okay, Mommy?" She asks me while we're walking up to the house.

Caston leans in and whispers to Brianna, "Mommy has baby

sniffles." I laughed through my tears when she looked at him like he had two heads.

She crosses her arms over her chest. "Well, I'll never get baby sniffles."

Caston puffs his chest out. "You're damn right you won't."

"Daddy said a bad word. Daddy said a bad word." She wiggles out of his hands and runs to the house where Jules has appeared on the patio.

Caston grabs my arm and stops me from continuing. He pulls me into his arms and places a kiss on my lips. I still get weak in my knees from his touch. Just then baby number two kicks.

"Oh boy, you just don't like when I get close to Mommy do you, little one?" He places his hands on my belly, feeling the movement.

"The calm before the storm," I state.

"You can always escape to the room if you need a break. I must insist when you do that you take me, though." He flashes me his sexy panty-dropping smile.

"Caston, you're naughty." I lean closer to his ear. "But I love you naughty, and you bet your ass I'll pull you with me."

I feel him harden at just the thought. "Easy there, cowboy, people should be here any minute."

No sooner did I say that than a mass of people come barreling out the door to come find us.

James, Rose, Sara, Jon, the kids, Beth, and Jake have arrived.

Beth and Jake tied the knot two years ago in the huge princess wedding that reminded me of my almost wedding. It took Beth a long time to agree to marry Jake. Not because she didn't love him, but she always said why ruin a good thing. She went on for months on how she didn't need that piece of paper to tell the world they were together. Jake didn't understand Beth's aversion to marriage. I eventually had to tell him, feeling like I was betraying my best friend. It should have been her telling him, but she was so hard headed, I knew she wouldn't. Jake went home that night and somehow got her to finally realize he wasn't going anywhere. I couldn't be happier for them. They make the cutest couple.

Caston completely made peace with James and Rose. The change in Rose is so uplifting. She has made so many strides to getting back to a 'normal' life. She still struggles with being away from home and being in crowds, but it's amazing how an active toddler can distract her. I'm happy because now my baby girl has a set of grandparents in her life, something I never had and didn't think was a possibility for Brianna. Rose has taken the roll of grandma to heart and spoils the kid rotten.

Sara and Jon are still going at it like rabbits. Their teenagers think it's gross when their parents kiss in public. If they only knew. I shake my head when the teens sit outside and immediately plug into whatever game is popular now. I am so not looking forward to when Brianna and number two are that age. Is it so bad for them to stay babies forever?

Jules has been doing duties of nanny when I can't be here. A lot has happened since the wedding.

Going back to Black Hollywood was great, but there was something missing each day. Even though I was pregnant, I worked out in the home studio every day. I even hired Professor Lee to come and help me work some of the muscles that needed to be re-trained. So many times I thought it was going to kill me. I'd cry at the end of our sessions, but what doesn't kill me makes me stronger.

Once Brianna was born, I didn't want to go back to Black Hollywood. I stayed home with her for a year. Then the day came when Caston came home to find me crying in the studio.

I was sitting in the middle of the studio with little Brianna toddling around the room in her little leotard and tutu. She was hanging on the bars and trying to put her little leg up on them just like I'd been doing before. Tears were falling down my face. I wasn't sure why I was so unhappy. I had the most amazing life. Perfect husband, amazing little girl, and anything I could ask for. When Caston walked in, he was immediately by my side.

"Bre, did you hurt yourself?"

He's touching my legs, looking over every inch trying to find the problem.

"No, Caston, I'm fine."

Sitting down he pulls me into his side. "Obviously, things aren't fine. Sabrina, you need to talk to me."

More tears fall down my face. "I'm not happy, Caston."

"With us?" I could tell he was hurt.

I move to straddle his lap. "No, Cass, we're fine. Something is missing for me, though."

Looking around the room, I chuckle as she runs toward us and slips falling on her little diaper butt.

"This, Caston," I gesture to the room, "I miss this."

"Dancing? But, Bre, you dance every day."

Taking his face in my hands I kiss him. "Caston, I just want more. I think I know how to do it, but I need your help."

He holds his hand out to accept Brianna into our little family circle. "You know I'll do anything for you."

"I want to open my own studio. I think that would help me. Since I can't dance, I could teach. Pass on my skills to others."

His face lights up. "Bre, that is a fantastic idea."

The very next day things were rolling to get Hollywood Stars up and running. It immediately took off. I was in heaven. It was exactly what was missing. Professor Lee helped me teach a few classes until I got established enough to get a staff. It didn't take long. Girls and boys were flocking to my studio. We have a waiting list and in only three years are looking to add another location.

Caston is still working hard at Black Hollywood, but Jon has taken over some more of the daily responsibilities because Caston decided he wanted to be home more with Brianna. It melted my heart that he wanted to be so hands on and actually took the initiative to follow through.

Beth started to work in the business side of my studio, so I could focus on teaching. So, I get to see her every day. I love it. Sara is still working at the club, and she couldn't be happier.

"Sabrina, everything okay?" Caston whispers in my ear, snapping me out of my day dream. I have the goofiest grin on my face.

"I'm more than perfect." Linking his arm, we head into the house.

The sun is setting and the lights around the pool turn on. I know it's getting close for the big surprise, but I'm trying to remain calm. Jules has made an amazing meal for us to celebrate Caston's and my four year anniversary. Taking our seats, I lean over and kiss Cass.

"Thank you, baby."

He smiles and stands. "Thank you everyone for being here. Not just today, but year after year. We are so blessed to have you all in our life and to share with you all our ups and downs. Thankfully, the last four years have been up." We all chuckle, knowing exactly what he is referring too.

"We have a few surprises planned tonight, but let's eat dinner before we get to them."

Smacking him lightly on his arm, I stand to take my place next to him. "We wanted to reveal what baby number two is going to be tonight."

Sara and Beth squeal, making me laugh. Jon just shakes his head, and Jake looks like he's about to puke at any minute.

"I hope you don't mind, but I'm going to start with dessert first."

Jules carries out a cake, and Brianna follows her out of the kitchen. Caston scoops her up, and we take the handle of the cake knife and cut in. Sliding out the piece, it's bright pink.

A large cheer goes up in the room, scaring Brianna, making her cry. Caston pulls her on to his shoulder, comforting her. I'm misty eyed again. He looks like he's going to burst with pride.

Engulfing me in a hug he whispers in my ear, "My girls." He kisses away my tears.

"This calls for a toast!" Caston cheers.

Everyone reaches for their champagne glasses, except Beth. I look over at Beth and know immediately before she says it, "No alcohol for me, thank you." Jake looks like he's ready to bust with pride.

"No way!" I shriek as I make my way around the table. She nods enthusiastically as I pull her up and wrap her in the biggest hug my swollen belly will allow.

"We're having a baby!" Jake says full of pride. Another round of cheers rise after his announcement.

"What a day," Caston says in my ear during dinner before pulling me for another kiss.

Once we are stuffed to the gills, fireworks start outside and everyone gets up to go watch them. Brianna slides off her booster seat and runs out ahead of everyone with Terrance on her heels. I turn to follow, but Caston stops me. Leading me down the hall to our bedroom instead, he's got that look on his face, and I immediately want him.

Locking the door behind me, he pulls me to him. "I want to make love to you under the fireworks."

I blush. "Caston, there are a ton of people here."

He strips off his clothes and begins taking mine off slowly. "No one can see up on our balcony. One of the best features of this room." He winks at me, and I let him lead me out to the outdoor bed.

Laying down he pulls me to straddle him. The slow motions and the excitement of being heard are too much, and I'm at the edge quickly. Once we're sated, I roll off him and Caston pulls up the sheets. We lay in each other's arms watching the rest of the fireworks before we must go back to our guests.

"Caston, can I ask you something?" I whisper.

His hand is stoking my belly mindlessly. "Of course."

"Are you upset the baby is another girl?" Holding my breath, I wait for his answer.

Not even skipping a beat he responds, "Bre, I wanted another girl. I'm thrilled."

I lean up on my elbow and look at him. "Really?"

The expression on his face is priceless. "Really. I love having Daddy's girls. I'm the luckiest guy in the world."

"We're lucky to have you. Thank you for making me your wife. I feel like we're still newlyweds, and that makes me happy. I don't ever want to get boring."

Caston laughs and kisses me taking my breath away. "I'll make sure that never happens. I love you Sabrina Marie Black. I love our little Brianna and..." he pauses.

"What?"

"Crap, we have to come up with another girl's name."

"What about Mya?" I ask.

"I love it." His smile evident.

He sits up and pulls me into his lap. "I love you, Brianna, and Mya. I'm lucky to have my girls."

Coming Fall, 2014
Beth & Jake's Novella

To stay up to date with FL Jacob and the
progress of her Work in Process:

www.fljacob.com
https://www.facebook.com/fljacob
www.twitter.com/fljacob

Acknowledgements

To my editor, Liz, with Book Peddler's Editing. You're awesome. What else can I say? You make my books better. That's all there is to it. You not only my editor, you are my friend and sometimes therapist. I can't thank you enough. Cheers to another book under our belt together and here's to the next one.

www.facebook.com/BookPeddlersEditing?ref=br_tf

To Michael & Dawn, with Digital Mitchall Event Photography and Rob, with Rob Miller Photography. When are we going to do the next shoot? You guys are so much fun. The professionalism and creative eye the three of you have took the cover picture to the next level. You took my idea and gave me a new one that was more than I even dreamed!

www.facebook.com/digitalmitchell

www.facebook.com/pages/Rob-Miller-Photography/296918773705422

To Kristine, once again, you were perfect! Thank you for enduring the hours of strange positions with your legs and feet. I don't think it

would have turned out as good without you.
www.facebook.com/pages/Kristine-Kowalski-NPC-Bikini-
Competitor/203007306535089

To Angela, with Fictional Formats. You do the job that I can't even wrap my brain around and I am thankful for your creative touches. You make my baby come to life artistically on the inside.
www.facebook.com/FictionalFormats

To all the blogs and Facebook pages who have helped promote me along the way. Thank you for all your hard work and dedication. I love getting to know you and working with everyone has been a dream. Thank you for treating little old me like a big deal.

To my followers. Your messages of support and love for Have I Told You got me through my slumps with writing this book. I appreciate all your help pimping my book to others. I write for you.

To all my beta readers, thank you for all of the constructive feedback you gave me to make my book better.

To Freddie Bonaire for the final once over. I appreciate your extra critical eye.

To Jen Leisenheimer for helping me with some last minute additions. You are my kindred spirit.

To my husband. Once again honey, I can't thank you enough for sticking with me through all the craziness. For being my rock. I hope I didn't neglect you too much. Love You!

To my little baby girls. Mommy loves you. Your smiles make everything worth it.

To anyone I may have forgotten, THANK YOU! I love you!

www.ingramcontent.com/pod-product-compliance
Lightning Source LLC
Chambersburg PA
CBHW072217170626
46813CB00003B/975